THE CUCKOO CLOCK MURDERS

An enthralling crime mystery full of twists

ROGER SILVERWOOD

Yorkshire Murder Mysteries Book 14

JOFFE BOOKS

Revised edition 2020
Joffe Books, London

First published in Great Britain as
***The Cuckoo Club Scam* 2009**

This book is a work of fiction. Names, characters, businesses, organisations, places and events are either the product of the author's imagination or are used fictitiously. Any resemblance to actual persons, living or dead, events or locales is entirely coincidental. The spelling used is British English except where fidelity to the author's rendering of accent or dialect supersedes this. The right of Roger Silverwood to be identified as author of this work has been asserted by him in accordance with the Copyright, Designs and Patents Act 1988.

Please join our mailing list for free Kindle books and new releases.

ISBN: 978-1-78931-404-5

CHAPTER 1

Sound Stage 2, Top Hat Film Studios, Oxspring Lane, Bromersley, South Yorkshire, UK. 1850 Hours. Monday 15 December 2008.

The make-up lady dropped the brush in the powder pot, unfastened the bib, whisked it away and said, 'That's it, Mrs Santana. Thank you.'

Felicity Santana eased her sylph-like body elegantly out of the chair and stepped out of the harsh lights of the make-up trailer into the huge expanse of the dimly lit sound stage. She looked across the array of viewing screens, cameras, microphones, playback projectors, screens, lighting standards and gathering of engineers, tradesmen and artists standing around and looking down at the set a hundred yards away, with the sky, moon and Plough shining brightly through a huge glass window.

Some of the crew nearby sensed her arrival, turned slightly, noted her presence and shuffled uneasily.

Three people made their way towards her through the clutter.

A young man wearing headphones round his neck said, 'Mrs Santana, Mr Isaacs sends his apologies and says about five minutes.' He dashed off.

'Can I get you anything, Mrs Santana?' Marianne Cooper, the gofer to the great star, said.

Felicity Santana didn't even acknowledge she was there.

'You look fantastic, Felicity,' a tall man with a shop-bought tan and a sugar-tongued voice said. 'Why don't we wait in your caravan? It's not very warm out here. Ridiculous … shooting summer scenes in winter without extra heating.'

She smiled up at him, turned to Marianne Cooper and said, 'A small gin with some fresh lime juice with ice. You'll find it in the bar behind the bookcase in my husband's office.'

Marianne Cooper smiled politely and ran off.

Felicity Santana and the man with the tan reached the caravan. As soon as the door was closed, he reached out to her, put his arms round her, whispered something indecent and kissed her gently on the lips.

She responded to the kiss and then they kissed again. He ran his hands down her back and her thighs. Her bosom heaved. She sighed and her fingers caressed the back of his neck. His face flushed and his heart beat soundly and rapidly like a tom-tom. After a few moments, she gently pushed him away with a smile. 'Not here. No. There's no time. I'll be called anytime.'

'When are you going to leave him?' he said, holding her head gently and looking into her eyes.

'When you have eighteen million pounds, darling,' she said.

He smiled. 'You can take his eighteen million and have a passion and love from me that that old man could never give you.'

She smiled and shook her head. 'Don't make assumptions, darling. Peter Santana is a very remarkable man.'

He put his hands under her arms, his thumbs under her bosom, looked into her eyes, wrinkled his eyebrows and said, 'You know that I can do a lot for you.'

She sighed. It was true, but she wasn't prepared to admit it to him.

'We talked about it once. I told you I could do it. All I would need would be … the means. I could get that. I have contacts. Might take a week or two.'

Her face glowed. She came very close to him. She ran her lips gently across his cheek. She ran her hands gently through his hair. Her mouth came up to his ear.

His heart began to pound again.

'If you were caught it would be twenty years,' she whispered.

'I wouldn't get caught. I wouldn't. I wouldn't.'

There was a knock at the door.

They separated quickly.

She reached down to the handle.

It was Marianne Cooper, the gofer, with a tumbler on a tray. 'Sorry to interrupt you, Mrs Santana,' she said with a smile.

Felicity Santana's eyes flashed. She glared down at the girl. 'You *didn't interrupt us*,' she snapped.

The gofer's eyes opened wide. The smile vanished. She was hurt and confused; it was impossible trying to get used to being treated rudely by 'stars'. She shrugged. 'Your drink. Fresh lime juice and gin.'

Mrs Santana snatched the glass from the tray and slammed the caravan door shut.

The man looked across at her, eyebrows raised. 'My,' he said, rubbing his chin, 'we *are* on edge tonight.'

'That girl saw us.'

'She couldn't have. The door was closed.'

'She suspects.'

'So what?'

'Can't risk any talk.'

He put his hand round her waist. 'Peter hasn't got long. He's seventy-two, heart disease. Then you'll be open season.'

'Huh,' she said, playing with his tie. 'How do you know? Doing what he's doing, he could go on for ever.'

'Sit down. Relax.'

She peeled his hand away from her tiny waist and walked the length of the caravan, carrying the glass, and then came back. She began to rub her chin, then remembered the make-up and looked at her fingers. She took a sip of the drink. 'He takes his pills, eats mostly fruit, doesn't smoke, doesn't touch alcohol, walks on the hills religiously for two hours every day; the rest of the twenty-four he spends in bed either writing or sleeping.'

'He comes here,' the man insisted.

'He comes here all right. For two hours. Comes in every month to view any new faces, count the money, and check that Isaacs isn't ordering too many paperclips.'

'Doesn't he ever go anywhere else?'

'Our mountain lodge at Tunistone, which I detest, and the hospital, for check-ups.' She pulled a face like a bottle of vinegar. 'Life is one big round of fun.'

There was a knock on the caravan door.

She leaned over and opened it.

It was the young man with the headphones. 'Mr Isaacs sends his compliments, Mrs Santana, and says that we are ready for you now.'

'Right,' she said.

The young man dashed off.

Mrs Santana finished off the drink with one swig, slammed the glass down, took a long look at herself in the fitted mirror and straightened her skirt.

The make-up lady with her bag was at one side of the door, and Marianne Cooper appeared at the other side.

Mrs Santana gave her the ringbinder holding her script, her keys and a spectacles case, then stepped out of the caravan, slammed the door, turned and led the procession down to the set.

The Farmhouse, Pennine Way, Tunistone, Near Bromersley, South Yorkshire, UK. 0010 Hours. Tuesday 16 December 2008.

A man came out of his dining room and into the hall on the ground floor of the modernized and extended farmhouse high in the Pennines. He was carrying a silver candelabra, which he put on the hall table. He struck a match and lit the three new pink candles. The flames flickered for a moment or two then settled. He then reached over the hall table up to a small box, which was screwed into the oak panelling on the wall. He took out several fuses, one at a time, until the crystal chandelier illuminating this end of the hall and situated almost above his head went out; he turned to see if the light in the room behind him, a downstairs bedroom, had also been extinguished. It had, so he closed the fuse box, then he took out his handkerchief and wiped clean each of the fuses he had withdrawn.

Then he picked up the candelabra and crossed the hall to the bedroom, causing huge shadows to balloon and swirl eerily on the bedroom wallpaper as he made his way to the nearest bed. He looked at the motionless mound down the middle of it and rubbed his chin. He held the candelabra over the pillow to show the collar of a pink nightdress and a hairy ear.

He shuddered as he looked down at the lifeless figure.

Then he heard a noise. The front door opened. Then closed.

He gasped. His blood froze. He wasn't expecting anyone. He shakily placed the candelabra on the bedside table, his pulse banging in his ears. He looked across at the bedroom door.

He swallowed with difficulty and called, 'Who's there?'

There was no reply.

His heart thumped as hard and as loud as a machine gun. He took a tentative step towards the bedroom door, then stopped when a man appeared in the doorway.

They recognized each other.

The intruder frowned when he saw the candelabra. 'What you up to, eh?'

'It's none of your business. You've no right to be here. Get out!' he said, advancing towards the intruder.

The other man screwed up his face like a paid bill, his eyes shining. 'That's the last time you talk to me like that,

Santana,' he said. Then he reached into his pocket, took out a handgun and pointed it at him.

'Get out,' Santana said. Then he saw the gun and remained motionless.

'Don't come any closer.'

'Don't point that at me unless you intend using it,' Santana said.

The man sneered at him and didn't hesitate. He fired once.

It hit Santana in the chest.

Santana put both hands up to the point of entry, his head dropped and he collapsed on the floor by the door.

The man stood over him, still holding out the gun. He saw blood ooze between Santana's fingers and grinned.

'At last, you bastard. I've got you at last,' he shouted as he kicked Santana's body violently in the side several times. Then the gunman bounced out of the room, closed the door, wiped the knob with his handkerchief and disappeared into the night.

DI Angel's Office, Bromersley Police Station, South Yorkshire, UK. 1000 hours. Tuesday 16 December 2008.

Detective Inspector Michael Angel was blowing the tune of 'We Three Kings Of Orient Are' through his teeth as he checked off and packed up paper files into a 'Heinz Tomato Soup' cardboard box. The papers all related to a case he had just solved, written up and was passing to the Crown Prosecution Service. It concerned a rich woman who had been abducted, robbed and murdered. The crime had been a totally callous affair and showed humanity at its meanest.

He was pleased to see the case closed for two reasons: the obvious one of taking another murderer off the streets and away from decent society, but also to reduce the bumf that tended to sit on his desk for much longer periods of time than he liked.

He pulled open his desk drawer and found a piece of string that was rolled up in a tidy figure of eight. He unfurled it, threaded it round the box, made a boy scouts' loop, tightened up the fastening, knotted it twice then held the box by the string and shook it. It seemed strong enough. He nodded favourably and put the box back on the desk.

There was a knock at the door. It was PC Ahmed Ahaz, aged twenty-one, who, as a probationer, came third at Aykley Heads Police College in Durham in 2006. Angel was very proud of him and considered him to be a first-rate copper. He was keen, personable and above average intelligence. He was carrying a handful of letters.

'Good morning, sir. Brought the post.' He put the letters on the desk.

'Right, Ahmed. Ta. Here, take this box of tricks round to Mr Twelvetrees at the CPS. He's expecting it.'

'Right, sir,' he said brightly.

Ahmed went out and closed the door.

Angel returned to the swivel chair, sat down at the desk, took a penknife out of the desk drawer and began to slit open the envelopes.

The phone rang. He reached out for it. 'Angel.'

It was Detective Superintendent Harker. He was talking as Angel put the phone to his ear, which annoyed Angel; he invariably missed the beginning of the sentence.

'A triple nine call, just in,' Harker said. 'A woman cleaner found the bodies of her employers in the bedroom of a converted farmhouse on the Pennines. She said that he was on the floor covered in blood and that his wife was in the bed, not moving. Sounds like a murder followed by a suicide. It is the country home of Peter Santana the TV producer and his actress wife Felicity. The address is The Farmhouse, Pennine Way, off Manchester Road, Tunistone. The cleaner said she'd wait there for you.'

The phone went dead.

The hairs on the back of Angel's neck turned to gooseflesh and his heart began to beat like a drum in the 1812.

He cleared the line then tapped a number into the handset. It was soon answered.

'Listen, Ahmed,' he said. 'In this order advise the following that there is a suspected murder and tell them I want them at the scene ASAP, all right?'

He then rattled off a list, gave him the Santanas' address and replaced the phone. He reached into the bottom drawer of his desk and took out a slim white packet containing a pair of rubber gloves, stuffed it in his pocket, picked up his coat and left the office.

The Farmhouse, Pennine Way, Tunistone, Near Bromersley, South Yorkshire, UK. 1045 hours. Tuesday 16 December 2008.

The Santanas were a high-profile couple internationally famous in the film and TV world. They lived in Bromersley, but took no interest in local activities. They had used the relatively insignificant South Yorkshire town as a convenient place to make films for the big and small screen. Although almost all Santana's films and TV dramas were shot inside the studio grounds, the old town buildings of Bromersley occasionally made an interesting backcloth, while the Pennine range of mountains, hills and woodlands nearby made for stunning scenery. In addition, labour was comparatively cheap and building land a tenth of the cost as the home counties.

Angel had heard of the Santanas and had seen pictures of the deliciously small Felicity Santana on TV from time to time. Her murder and that of her husband would make prominent news in the entertainment world abroad as well as throughout the UK.

The Santanas' farmhouse was large and had been modernized, with several additional rooms built on at ground floor level, to bring it up to Santana's requirements. It was high up on the Pennines off the main road between Sheffield and Manchester, and Angel wondered how they would have managed to reach the place in the heavy, snowy days of winters past.

He pointed the bonnet of the BMW up the hundred yards steep climb, then followed the track right, along a short level stretch up to open gates to a short drive, where he pulled up thirty yards away from the front door. Ahead of him were parked a small foreign red car and a big new silver Mercedes.

He switched off the ignition and got out of the car.

At that moment, he was pleased to see a white van from SOCO at Bromersley drive up behind him. Inside it was the team of specialist investigators led by DS Donald Taylor. It parked up behind the BMW.

He gave them a wave of acknowledgement as he made his way towards the house.

Before he reached the front door, it was suddenly opened and a woman in a blue overall rushed out and made straight for him. 'I have never seen anything like it,' she said. She was panting. 'I am the one who dialled 999. Never seen anything like it. You are from the police, aren't you?'

'Detective Inspector Angel,' he said, quietly. 'May I ask your name?'

'Gloria Totty. Mrs,' she said.

'Are you all right?'

'Yes, thank you. Am I pleased to see you! I helped myself to a big drop of their brandy while I was waiting for you. They wouldn't have begrudged it, I don't think. Never seen anything like it, Inspector. I'm the housekeeper here.'

'What exactly have you seen, Mrs Totty?'

'Mr Santana dead as anything, blood all over. And Mrs Santana dead in bed. I didn't go near her.'

DS Taylor joined them, togged up in a white sterile suit, headcover, green boots and rubber gloves.

He looked at Angel then the woman.

'Mrs Totty,' Angel said. 'Which room are they in?'

She pointed towards the front door. 'Bedroom. First on the left.'

'Downstairs?'

'Yes.'

'Thank you,' Angel said.

Taylor nodded at Angel and rushed inside the house. Three others similarly clad, carrying rolls of plastic foam, followed.

'Now tell me what exactly happened, Mrs Totty. You say you are the housekeeper here?'

'Part-time, yes. Ever since they bought the place and had it converted. Start at ten, finish at three today. I arrived at around ten this morning. I knew they were here because his car—' She pointed to the big silver Mercedes, '—was there. Unusual, though, because he always puts it in the garage. And they don't come up here much, this time of the year. Well, she doesn't come up at all, anyway, now. Well, I let myself in. I have a key.'

'The door was locked?'

She put her hand to her chin, rubbed it and said, 'There's a thing. No, Inspector. As a matter of fact it wasn't locked, no.'

'Please go on.'

'I went into the kitchen, his study, the sitting room and the big lounge … the gymnasium … and there was no sign of life. I knew he wouldn't be in the swimming pool this time of year. I didn't call out or anything. I guessed he'd be in bed tapping into his laptop. He has it fitted up with a table so that he can swing it across. Mr Santana liked everything quiet, like, especially when he was writing. No radio, no Hoover, nothing like that. I made a pot of tea. He always enjoyed a drink of tea. Took it to the bedroom. Knocked on the door. No reply. Again, still no reply. Opened it and … oh dear.' She shivered and rubbed her arms.

The sun was shining and there was no breeze, but it was not warm.

'Sit in here,' he said. 'We can talk in here.' He opened the car door for her.

As Mrs Totty got in, he looked round. The site was now a place of concerted activity. Dr Mac, the pathologist, had arrived. DS Ron Gawber's car was pulling up behind him. The SOCO team were taking specialist dust-sucking machines into the house. The mortuary wagon was parking on some space in front of the big garage, and a young constable was putting up police signs down the drive.

Angel walked round to the other side of the car and opened the door. When they were both settled he said, 'Now, what did you find in the bedroom?'

She swallowed. 'It was Mr Santana. He was on the floor in front of the door. His face was grey with an expression of pain, but fixed, frozen like a black and white photograph. I knew he was dead. There was blood on his shirt, his hands, pullover, everywhere.'

'And Mrs Santana?'

'Unusual, that. She hasn't been here since there was a leak in the swimming pool and the builders were brought in. Must be five years ago. I didn't go any further into the room. She was in bed. Never moved. Even when I screamed. Must certainly be dead. Bit of a nightie and back of her head showing. Horrible.'

He blew out a sigh. 'Anything been moved?'

'Yes. There was a candelabra at the side of the bed. And the candles were still lit. We never light them. I don't understand it. They were just for show.'

Angel rubbed his chin.

'There must have been some trouble with the lights,' she added. 'The fuse box in the hall is open and some fuses pulled out and put on the table.'

'Anything else?'

She shook her head. 'Don't think so.'

A mobile phone rang. It was Angel's. He wasn't pleased. He pulled a face and dived into his pocket. 'Excuse me,' he said and opened it up. It was the superintendent.

'Yes, sir?' he said into the phone.

'Ah, Angel,' Harker said. 'Correction. It can't be Felicity Santana dead in that bedroom. She's just been on the phone to our reception, alive and kicking, reporting her husband missing. The telephonist put her on to me and I told her about the triple nine call from her housekeeper up there. She now understands that her husband is dead and that there is an unidentified woman in her bed. She is understandably extremely upset.'

Angel blinked and pulled a face like he'd caught the smell of the gravy at Strangeways.

'And she's on her way up to you,' Harker added mischievously.

Angel's lip tightened momentarily against his teeth, then he said, 'Right sir,' He was furious, he hadn't yet had the opportunity to see either of the two corpses or check out their identities.

There was a click and the phone went dead.

Angel snapped the mobile shut and shoved it in his pocket.

'Sorry about that, Mrs Totty.'

She nodded understandingly.

He was wondering what to tell her when Dr Mac, in his whites, arrived outside the BMW and tapped on the window.

Angel lowered it.

Mac pulled down his mask and said, 'Excuse me, Michael.' He looked pale and unusually agitated. He glanced at Mrs Totty then looked back at Angel. 'You'd better come and … have a look at this … for yourself'. I can't explain.'

Angel frowned. He had never seen Mac acting so strangely. He was not a man who usually found words difficult.

Angel got out of the car, leaving Mrs Totty open mouthed. He remembered the rubber gloves, tore open the packet and pulled them on. Then he nodded at the doctor, who hurried along, keeping to the plastic pathway laid by SOCO, through the front door, down the short hall to the open bedroom door.

Mac pointed to the heap on the floor covered in sterile plastic sheeting. 'Peter Santana,' he said.

Angel looked round. There were splashes of blood on the door, the door frame, the carpet and the wallpaper. He reached down and pulled up the plastic. The dead man was flat on his back on the Chinese carpet. He was slim, short and fully dressed in a suit, shirt, tie and black leather shoes. There was blood everywhere, particularly around the chest area. Angel took a close look at his face. The eyes were closed and a pair of spectacles were on the carpet next to him.

Angel wrinkled his nose and sighed as he lowered the plastic sheeting.

He looked at Mac who, with the nod of his head, invited him to follow him further into the room. He pointed to a silver candelabra, draped in melted pink wax with three candle stubs in it, on a bedside table.

'That was still lit when I came in here.'

Angel rubbed his chin.

'And there's no electricity in the place.'

'What? Why?'

Mac shrugged.

Angel shuddered. He realized the room was cold. It was also eerie.

Mac then pointed to the nearer of two large beds; SOCO had covered the bedspread and pillows with sterile sheeting. A mound down the middle, however, suggested there was a body, alive or dead, underneath.

Mac went up to the head of the bed and Angel stood next to him. He wondered what was so special that he should be specially brought in before Mac and SOCO had finished their initial examinations. If it was something grotesque, he reckoned he had seen everything.

He steeled himself as Mac, with a rubber-gloved finger and thumb, gently peeled back the plastic sheeting covering the pillows to reveal the pretty collar of a silk garment covering a pink hairy ear. He then pulled back the bedclothes until it became clear that the body wearing a woman's nightdress was that of a dead pig.

CHAPTER 2

DI ANGEL'S OFFICE, BROMERSLEY POLICE STATION, SOUTH YORKSHIRE, UK. 1400 HOURS. TUESDAY 16 DECEMBER 2008.

Felicity Santana parked her racy new Jaguar next to Angel's in the police station car park and then accompanied him, causing a great buzz of excitement and a shower of testosterone from the men, gliding through reception and down the green corridor. The WPCs looked with interest and envy as she passed them by. Everybody noticed her great beauty and many remarked afterwards on how small she appeared to be in real life.

Angel closed the office door, made Felicity Santana as comfortable as possible in his little office and then settled himself down in his chair behind the desk.

'I'm all right now, thank you, Inspector,' she said, pushing a moist tissue back into her handbag. 'I'm a tough bird. It takes more than the death of my husband and the knowledge that after ten years of marriage he had an unusual predilection for a pig … to floor me.'

Angel pursed his lips. 'I am sure that is not the case, Mrs Santana.'

‘A pig. It’s disgusting. What sort of a person will people think I have been married to? I would rather have had Peter caught in bed with a pretty, young actress. Dammit, there are plenty of those who would have been glad to have obliged. I could have dealt with *that*. It would have been simple competition. But I can’t compete with a pig. Just think what the tabloids will make of that, Inspector? My God. They’re going to have one hell of a party when that comes out.’

She sighed and shook her head.

He nodded sympathetically.

‘There are some questions …’ he said.

‘Of course. Let’s get it over with. I’m bound to be the chief suspect. Young wife. Successful actress. Married ten years to world-famous multi-millionaire producer and writer, Peter Santana. Co-respondent, a pig. I’m here to be shot at, Inspector. Fire away.’

‘Was your husband at all interested in pigs? Was there something pointed about the animal being a pig, do you think? Did your husband have any interests in animals at all?’

‘None at all, Inspector.’

‘Was he into “Save the whale” or “Stop puppy farming” or anything like that?’

‘No.’

‘Did he support any animal charity?’

‘No.’

‘Did you have any pets? Cats or dogs?’

‘Not a flicker of interest in them, Inspector. All the years I’ve known him. No. Not even a goldfish. I find this pig business utterly unbelievable. Dammit. He didn’t even eat meat anymore.’

‘He was a vegetarian?’

‘Only since his heart attack.’

‘Oh. It wasn’t to save the species or…?’

‘It was to save Peter Santana, Inspector.’

He stifled a smile.

‘No interest in anthropology?’

'Not unless it was profitable, or you could make a film about it.'

'Your husband was a great writer. He's written some best-selling books which have been made into blockbuster films. Could this pig in a bed have anything to do with a plot he was working on?'

'My husband could – in his imagination – have written about a human couple being miniaturized to the size of microbes, strapped to a bee's leg and deposited next day into the flower of a hollyhock without even moving from his laptop, so I am damned certain that he didn't need to get a pig into his bed to heighten his imagination.'

Angel shook his head. He was getting nowhere.

'How do *you* explain it, then, Mrs Santana? A pig dressed in a nightdress in …'

'I can't, Inspector. I can't. He's never done anything like this before. Although Peter wrote some highly original fiction, he was essentially a practical man with his feet firmly on the ground. He was a businessman first and a creative man second. He simply had the skill or the luck to create and produce what people wanted to see and hear. He understood entertainment, when so many writers and producers did not.'

Angel decided on another tack. 'He was working on something?'

She sighed. 'He was *always* working on something. I don't know what it was.'

'He was writing for you?'

'There would probably have been a major part in it for me, yes. Ever practical was Peter. Keep the money in the family, you know.'

'What was it about?'

'I don't know. He never spoke about it until it was finished. I would be the first to read it. He valued my opinion. He didn't always act on it, but I flatter myself that he was always interested to know what I thought.'

'About your own part, or the whole thing?'

'Both. Naturally I was interested in the character that he had written for me, but that wasn't it all. I wanted to know what the thing was all about.'

'So you have no idea what your husband was writing?'

'Sorry.'

Angel knew that there was a highly skilled computer team from specialist police agencies that he could call on; they could soon review Santana's latest writing and see if it related in any way to a pig in a nightdress in a bed.

'I suppose some other person could have put the pig in your bed.'

She nodded. 'I can't think who.'

She suddenly looked up and blinked thoughtfully several times. 'You know, Inspector, Peter was not very strong. He was seventy-two, had heart disease. He thought he hadn't long to live. Did an hour in the gym and walked an hour or more every day. He was determined to regain some of his strength after his heart attack. I don't know the weight of that pig, but I doubt very much if he could have carried it by himself.'

Angel wrinkled his nose. 'That we may never know, Mrs Santana. And there is the business of the nightdress. The pig was dressed in a nightdress. Putting a dead weight of a pig into a nightdress would have been quite a job, I must say. That may have been a job for two people. We'll see.'

She held up her hands and shrugged.

'Can I have the name of your husband's GP?'

'Of course. Dr Prakash. Very good man. He has a surgery on Bond Road.'

'Thank you,' he said, scribbling the name on an envelope taken from his inside pocket. He looked up and said, 'Would you say you had a happy marriage, Mrs Santana?'

'As happy as most people,' she replied.

Angel noticed that there was a slight tightening then relaxing of the lips. She clearly didn't like the question.

Angel rubbed the lobe of his ear between finger and thumb.

'I know what you're thinking,' she said. 'The difference in our ages.'

'That's a start. Mr Santana was seventy-two. I won't ask you *your* age.'

'I'm forty-two,' she said boldly. She was only small, but she was very confident about her looks.

Angel said: 'And you look younger.'

'Thank you. I have taken care of myself. And that's why I am still in work and at the top of my profession. Some people would say that it was because I was Peter's wife. I don't deny that it helped, but Peter was such a man, Inspector, that if there had been somebody he had preferred in any part in any film he had written, he would have had her in and cut me out without a second thought.'

'But that never happened?'

'No.'

'Your husband was a very wealthy man. Do you know how he left his will?'

'I certainly do, Inspector. Nothing complicated. Nothing tedious. He left everything to me.'

Angel blinked. She had said it quickly, smoothly, unemotionally, like a scalpel cutting through an umbilical cord.

He narrowed his eyes then licked his lips before he said, 'I need to ask you about your movements and your husband's movements yesterday.'

'Certainly. Nothing very interesting, I can tell you, Inspector. We were at our house on Creesforth Road in Bromersley. We sleep in separate bedrooms these days. Peter doesn't sleep very well, so that when he is awake he might tap away at his laptop that he has on a table he can swivel across the bed. He was working at that when the studio car arrived to collect me at 7.45 that morning. I knew our housekeeper would arrive at nine o'clock. He seemed happy enough when I called out, as I left the house. I did my stint at the studio. Everything went well. Got back home about one o'clock. Peter was up and dressed. Had lunch with him in the kitchen. It was only fruit and coffee. He asked how the shooting had gone. I told him. I reminded him that I would be out that evening – provided the sky stayed clear – for the night scene. He said he would remember. Then we began to discuss domestic matters … staff arrangements for Christmas. His PA arrived in the middle of it. He took his apple into his study with her. Then a man from the accountants called. Then the phone began ringing; it seemed non-stop. I finished my lunch and carried on with my own work. I had some lines to learn and rehearse for the night's shoot.'

'Was all that usual?'

'Oh yes. Everybody wanted to see Mr Santana. He was quite masterful at seeing only those people he wanted to see. His PA was good at marshalling everybody. At about three o'clock, it quietened down, and he came out of the study into the kitchen. I was talking about Christmas with the housekeeper. He grunted the usual thing about going to bed to write, took a bottle of his favourite water out of the fridge and went upstairs.' She sighed then bit her lip. 'That was the last I saw of him.'

'Why was he out at Tunistone? Did he go there to write or what?'

'I don't know. It's very odd. Completely out of character. When I left at six o'clock, it was pitch black, of course. I thought Peter would stay there in bed, either writing or sleeping, or reading or watching TV for the evening. I expected him to stay in his bedroom for the entire night. When I came home at about eleven o'clock, his room was in darkness, so I assumed he was asleep.'

'Did you did notice his car was missing?'

'No. I was brought home in a studio car. I didn't go in the garage.'

'So you thought he was in the house asleep?'

'Yes, and I didn't know otherwise until about 9.30 this morning. I took a tray of tea into his room and he wasn't there. I was very surprised. It was completely out of character. I phoned the studio first. Spoke to William Isaacs. He knew nothing. Then I phoned his PA. She usually knows what's going on, but she knew nothing. I never thought he would be at Tunistone. He's fallen out of favour with the place lately and was thinking of buying somewhere in a warmer climate. Even when I discovered that his car had gone, it didn't occur to me that he might be up there … not at this time of the year anyway. I waited a little while. I didn't want to make a complete fool of myself. Then when he didn't turn up and I had run out of ideas, I phoned the police station. The rest you know.'

Angel nodded, not to convey that he was in agreement. There was a lot he didn't know. But he thought it was a good point at which to break off.

'You wanted me, sir?' Angel said at the door.

He noticed a strong smell of Vick. There was often a pong of a menthol medicament in Detective Superintendent Harker's office.

'Yes. Shut the door,' he said. 'Keep the warmth in, for goodness' sake.'

Angel noticed Harker's nose was red and his forehead perspiring. If he had a cold or flu, he didn't want it. Angel was determined to keep as far away from him as possible.

Harker reached out for an A4 sheet of paper in a wire basket on the desk in front of him. It looked like an inter-office memo.

'Sit down. What I have to tell you is very important and highly confidential.'

Angel undid his jacket pocket and sat down on the chair facing the desk.

Harker cleared his throat and looked up from the memo. 'Now then,' he said. 'You know the chief constable has just returned from an ACPO meeting in Northampton?'

Angel didn't know. He didn't care, but he nodded so that Harker would move on.

'Well, there was a big noise from the Home Office there. He dropped something privately to the chief … He didn't want to overstate the case, but … there are forged ten-Euro notes floating about the north of England. They are being picked up all over Europe, causing the Bank of England no end of difficulties. They are quite excellent forgeries, superficially. No rubbish. Difficult for the man in the street to detect at first sight. Perfectly printed. Works of art. However, they have no watermarks or metal strips, and they are not numbered progressively, so a simple examination will detect them. Now, Bromersley seems to be geographically in the centre of where the counterfeit currency is distributed. If it is so, you can see that it is very embarrassing for us. The Home Office don't want the media to get hold of it. So it must be kept low key. The bank doesn't want our partners in Europe to become aware of it either, not until we have traced the source and closed the printing press down. All right? The forgeries are driving the Bank of England crackers. Euros are no use at a retail level on the UK mainland, of course, but exceedingly useful in travel agents, banks and so on.'

'Anything to go on, sir?'

Harker's bushy eyebrows went up. 'I've told you all there is.'

Angel had never heard of currency forgeries in Bromersley before. He had once arrested a man forging sovereigns out of melted-down wedding rings. It was hardly profitable for the old lag because it took him too long to produce examples good enough to be passed. Paper currency, however, was something else. Once set up, huge quantities could be quickly counterfeited, limited only by the accessibility of suitable paper and ink.

He shrugged; he couldn't see how he could initiate any inquiries without a specific report where the forged stuff had actually changed hands.

Minimally, such an enterprise these days needed an underground printing press with photographic resources, a skilled printer, or an eager amateur with the ability to match ink colours, plus some sort of a distribution set-up. The location could be anywhere, but he couldn't think of any possible culpable party at that moment. He wrinkled his nose. He couldn't get into all that. He had a murder on his hands, a very peculiar murder. And murder was his business.

'Right, sir,' Angel said and stood up to leave.

'Just a minute,' Harker said.

Angel sat down.

'How are you getting along with that Santana case?'

Angel pursed his lips. He knew the super of old. This could be a trick question.

'Straightforward, is it?' Harker added, looking at him with one eye slightly closed.

Angel wondered what Harker was getting at. 'Too early to say, sir,' he said cautiously.

'I see that you've got a pig in the case.'

Angel thought he detected the beginning of a smile from the man. That could be dangerous. Harker was not inclined to smile and when he did, something calamitous always happened. Last time, it was July last year. There was the big flood and almost a hundred Bromersley residents became homeless overnight. Nevertheless, he would have to answer him.

'A dead pig *was* found in Peter Santana's bed, sir.'

'Dressed in a nightdress?' Harker said. 'Why? What for? What's the sense in it?'

'At the moment, sir, I have no idea,' Angel said.

The smile didn't develop.

'Come in,' Angel called.

'Yes, sir?'

It was DC Edward Scrivens, an eager young man, twenty-four, who had been a detective two years now. Angel thought he would do well.

'Aye. Come in, Ed,' he said. 'I want you to gather together all the computers, laptops, hard disks, floppy disks, and memory sticks that Peter Santana had used during the past month or so. You'll need to go to the Top Hat Film Studios, his house on Creesforth Road and the farmhouse place in Tunistone. I've got some computer geeks coming over from Special Services in Wakefield. They are going to check on Santana's work to see if there is anything in the computers that might help us. All right?'

'Right, sir,' he said, making for the door.

'Follow it through. And let me know what they find ASAP.'

'Right, sir.'

'When the Wakefield lads have finished, see that any kit we don't need for evidence goes back to where it came from. All right?'

As Scrivens went out, Gawber came in.

'There are still wholesale butchers around in spite of all the supermarkets,' Gawber said. 'There's a man runs a small business using an old cold store that was part of the abattoir at Dodworth Bottom. Supplies pubs, cafés, hotels, places like that.'

'What did he know about the pig?'

'He got a phone call from a man in the middle of last week inquiring about a whole pig. The butcher thought it was for roasting on a spit. He sells one or two in the summer sometimes to members of the public.'

'Was it Santana?'

'Didn't give his name. A thin, frail, white-haired man, he said, in a very smart suit, collected it, paid cash. Had it put in the boot of his car, a Mercedes.'

'That would be him. Anything else?'

'It had to be fresh. Seemed fussy about the weight. Had to weigh a hundred pounds, apparently.'

Angel frowned. 'A good round number, I suppose. Anything else?'

'No, sir.'

With a furrowed brow, Angel rubbed his chin. 'Why would anybody in their right mind dress a pig in a silk nightdress and tuck it in his bed?'

'I suppose it *was* Santana who dressed the pig in the nightdress?'

'Well, he was the one who bought the pig, wasn't he?'

The two men looked at each other.

Angel said: 'It doesn't make sense. Have you seen what a beautiful woman his wife is?'

Gawber's face brightened. 'Oh *yes*, sir.'

'And being a big film producer,' Angel said, 'his wife said that there have always been women eager to throw themselves at him – starlets, wannabes. I bet that was true. These days everybody wants to be famous, but not because they're brilliant at what they do.'

'That's why I think it must be some sort of a deviant practise,' Gawber said. 'He couldn't find anybody willing to do something outrageously abnormal or indecent enough for him for money.'

Angel frowned. 'It's a *dead* pig, Ron. Let's stay real. I could have introduced him to a dozen or more lasses we've had through here in the last twelve months.'

'Well, maybe he wanted a man, sir?'

Angel ran his hand through his hair. 'No, Ron. If we go down that road, we'll have to bring psychologists and all sorts of experts in to get under our feet. Let's try common sense first. Let's find out where he got the glamorous nightdress from.'

'Want *me* to try and do that, sir?'

'Aye. There's a shopping bag and wrapping in the waste at the farmhouse from that big lingerie shop, on Market Street. Exotica, I think it's called. I should try there first.'

Gawber made for the door.

'And if you see Trevor Crisp in your travels,' Angel said, 'tell him I want him, smartish.'

Gawber nodded and went out.

Angel reached out for the phone. He tapped in a number. He was ringing the pathologist.

Dr Mac answered the phone.

'What you got, Mac? What did Santana die of?'

Mac grunted. He wasn't pleased. 'Oh, it's you, Michael. Might have known. What do ye think I am?' he protested. 'I'm not gifted with second sight. I haven't even started the PM yet.'

'Come on, Mac. Don't mess about. What does it *look* like?'

'Obviously murder. One gunshot to the heart.'

'Did you get any samples from the scene?'

'No.'

'Anything else?'

'Nothing useful to you, I am thinking. Now can I have ma tea?'

'Thanks, Mac. That's great. Won't keep you. Now what about the pig?'

The doctor sniffed. 'Aye. What about it?' he said sharply. 'You're not expecting me to carry out a post mortem on a pig, are ye?'

Angel stifled a smile. 'No. But you have had a look at it?'

'Aye. And it was a good, fresh, female beastie.'

'Was the pig complete?' Angel said.

'Complete? *Complete?* You mean had it been gutted or whatever they do with pigs?' Mac said quickly with a raised voice.

'Yes?'

'Apart from a great loss of blood from a butcher's cut at the throat, it was sound in every particular.'

'Were there any wounds at all on the pig? I was thinking of gunshot wounds, for instance?'

'Certainly not, and that's all I have to say on the matter.'

'It had been refrigerated?'

'Yes. It had been refrigerated, and if you need to know anything else, you need to apply to the Fatstock Marketing Board or bring in a veterinarian. You have exhausted my knowledge on dead pigs.'

'Thank you, Mac.'

There was a loud click as the doctor replaced his phone.

Angel rubbed his chin. He seemed to have ruffled Mac's feathers. He regretted it. He got on well with the doctor who had been pathologist at Bromersley for more than fifteen years. He liked him because he was good at his job and was to be relied on absolutely in the witness box.

He reached into a drawer and pulled out the telephone directory. He was looking for the number of Doctor Prakash, Peter Santana's GP. He remembered he was on Bond Street. He soon found the number. He got through to the doctor and told him about the death of Santana.

'I am extremely sorry to hear that, Inspector,' the doctor said. 'I am both surprised and shocked.'

'I would like to speak to you further about him, Doctor.'

'Of course. When would you like to come?'

'As soon as possible.'

'Come round right away.'

Ten minutes later, Angel was in Doctor Prakash's surgery.

'Thank you for seeing me so promptly. What I need to know firstly, Doctor, is the general health of Peter Santana.'

'Well, he had an inoperable heart condition. A leaking valve. He needed a replacement. He might have survived the operation, but perhaps not any rejection, which initially always happens. Also it was felt that he would not have had the strength to survive any infection, which is also common. However, all his other major functions were working perfectly well, therefore it was thought that, with careful management, he may have survived another two or ten or even twenty years. His changed lifestyle, diet and exercise routines were rigorously maintained, and his physical strength was increasing every time I saw him. For a small, elderly man he was quite strong, and the prognosis was satisfactory.'

'When did you last see him?'

'I see him quite often.' Prakash looked down at his notes. 'The tenth of this month, only a week ago.'

Angel's eyebrows went up. He nodded. 'And what was he like?'

'He was very unusual, Inspector. Always polite and quietly spoken. Clear thinking. Decisive. Tremendously industrious.'

'A busy man?'

'I suppose it was necessary for a man to become so successful?'

Angel pursed his lips and blew out a length of air.

'His wife, Felicity … she is also a patient of yours, Doctor. What can you tell me about her?'

'Nothing much. Hardly ever saw her. She seems to enjoy rude health. A lot younger than Peter, of course.'

'How would you sum *her* up?'

Prakash thought for a moment, then smiled. 'Like her husband,' he said, 'except that she was more excitable and tended to speak forthrightly.'

'Were you ever consulted by either or both of the couple on any matters that may have arisen due to the significant difference in their ages?'

The doctor considered his answer carefully. 'No. But I must say, Inspector, if they had, I would not have been willing to discuss the matter with you. But I repeat, they did not.'

Angel shook his head and said, 'A strange thing has happened in this case, Doctor Prakash. It is bound to come out in the newspapers, so there is no necessity to keep it secret. When the fully dressed body of Peter Santana was found on the floor in the bedroom of his house in Tunistone, in the bed was a dead pig, a 100 lb sow, dressed in a pink silk nightdress. I can't make any sense of it. As Mr Santana's GP, can you offer any kind of explanation?'

Prakash's eyes glowed. He was clearly amazed. 'No, I cannot.' Then he added, 'Of course, the pig is an offensive symbol in the Jewish faith.'

'That's right, but Peter Santana was not Jewish…. Anyway, we know that he bought the pig himself.'

Prakash shook his head. 'Really? I am sorry, Inspector. I can't throw any light on the matter.'

CHAPTER 3

The Fisherman's Rest Public House, Canal Road, Bromersley. 2100 hours. Tuesday 16 December 2008.

It was a filthy night, and colder than a Strangeways lavatory seat. The gusty wind and hard-driven rain made the outdoor Christmas lights rattle next to the wall and the flickering pub sign. Inside the Fisherman's Rest, things were very quiet. Being the week before Christmas, it was thought that some of the usual drinkers were holding back in anticipation of the annual blow-out, while others were simply conserving funds. Inflation had increased the cost of Christmas presents, cards, food and decorations and so on. In addition, trade had dropped considerably since it became illegal to smoke tobacco in a public place.

The landlord, Clem Bailey, who was also the licensee, barman, waiter, pot washer, cellarman, lavatory cleaner, floor sweeper, bouncer and occasional sandwich maker was making a poor living. At that very moment, he was standing behind the bar, hand in chin, scanning the room and wondering whether he was contravening any health and safety regulations, local council bye-laws, hygiene rules, fire regulations, licensing, gambling, singing or dancing laws. He was also monitoring the door to keep out minors, prostitutes, tinkers, bookies' runners and other undesirables. He was always at risk of losing his licence. To stay in business he had to create a welcoming environment for the customers, obey the laws, keep sweet with the police, observe all the bye-laws, and sell gallons of beer.

In one corner of the Fisherman's Rest was a gathering of four men, quietly drinking and occasionally talking in subdued voices among themselves. In another badly lit corner, there was a courting couple sitting as close to each other as Siamese twins. Then there were two men at a table at the back, and a party of five, three women and two men, at a table in the centre. Thirteen altogether. Not a lucky number.

Suddenly, a short recurring clicking sound came from the mechanism of an unusual-looking clock on the wall, in the shape of a tiny chalet with a pendulum swinging underneath it and two chains hanging down with weights at the ends. A moment later, the two tiny doors of the chalet opened and a small piece of polished wood with a plastic beak and some feathery appendage popped out on a spring and went back again at great speed. At each appearance, one heard the crude mechanical sound of a cuckoo. It appeared nine times.

Most of the customers ignored the noise; some looked up and frowned, a few smiled.

The pub door banged and out of the wind and rain came a big man. He was wearing a woollen hat pulled well down over his ears and a woollen scarf across his mouth. He stood by the door, looked round the room, then hesitated a moment as he spotted a particular face among the four men in the corner. He turned quickly away, walked up to the bar and began to loosen his wet leather gloves.

Bailey looked up, took in the hat and scarf and said, 'Nasty weather.'

The man stared at him but didn't reply.

Bailey looked up again at the half-covered face. 'Can I get you anything?'

'A pint of bitter,' the man said.

Bailey selected a glass, pulled the pint and placed it on a coaster.

'And a beef sandwich,' the man added.

Bailey then went out through the door behind the bar to the tiny kitchen to make the sandwich. He took a plate from the cupboard, selected two slices of bread, took the lid off the butter dish and reached out for a knife.

Then, in quick succession, Bailey heard three gunshots. A woman screamed. Somebody shouted.

Bailey's stomach leaped up to his mouth. He dropped the butter knife and turned towards the door to the bar.

The pub door banged shut.

Bailey rushed up to the bar counter. There was the sickly smell of cordite.

One of the four men in the corner was slumped over the table; the other three were standing, staring down at him. One of them pulled him up by his shoulder to see his face. Blood was streaming out of a wound to his temple. When the man saw it, he gasped and gently lowered the injured man back to the table.

In the cold silence, somebody said, 'Oh my God.'

The courting couple, who were standing and holding on to each other, leaned over to see the wounded man.

Bailey looked across at the bleeding man and said, 'What happened? What the *hell* happened?'

The man nearest to the injured man said, 'He's hurt bad. That man shot him. Just like that. He shot him.'

'Oh hell,' Bailey said. He rubbed his chin.

'He's dead,' the man cried, his lips trembling.

Another man said, 'There's a pulse. I can feel it.'

Bailey reached for the phone and tapped out 999.

The five people at the table in the middle stood up, picked up some shopping bags and went quietly out of the door, quickly followed by the two men nearby, who drank up and left.

Bailey's hand was shaking. He called into the phone: 'Ambulance. And police.'

The door closed. He looked up. The courting couple had also gone.

'Right, Ed,' Angel said. 'In your own words, just tell me what happened.'

DC Edward Scrivens, a young detective on Angel's team, said, 'Well, sir, last night I got a call following a triple nine at 2105 hours to go to the Fisherman's Rest. When I arrived an injured man, Vincent Doonan, was being taken out by two ambulance men and whisked off to the General Hospital. He's very badly wounded and is still in theatre having surgery. The witnesses were only able to say that a big man dressed in black coat, scarf and woolly hat came into the pub, ordered from the bar, then pulled out a handgun and fired three shots at the man, then rushed out.'

Angel listened carefully, nodded, wrinkled his nose and said, 'You advised SOCO?'

'Yes, sir. They are at the scene now.'

Angel rubbed his chin.

'When did you last speak to the hospital?'

'Must be half an hour ago now, sir. He was still with us.'

'Next of kin?'

'I don't know, sir. I don't know where he lives. One of the witnesses thinks he lives on Edward Street, but he doesn't know what number. I haven't had time to look it up.'

Angel nodded then pursed his lips. 'Have you had any sleep?'

'No, sir.'

'Right, lad. Leave me those names and addresses and then push off.'

Scrivens smiled. It had been a long night. He tore a sheet off a notepad, handed it to him and went out.

Angel sat down, glanced at the list of witnesses, stuffed it in his pocket, reached out for the phone and tapped in a number.

There was a knock at the door. It was Detective Sergeant Trevor Crisp.

Crisp was considered to be the glamour boy of the team. He was a handsome man, unmarried, and was known to have had a few near misses with WPC Leisha Baverstock, the station beauty. He was never around, impossible to find and a master of excuses. He was also an expert at trying Angel's patience.

Angel glared up at him. He sighed. 'Ah,' he said and replaced the phone. 'The Scarlet Pimpernel.'

'You wanted me, sir?'

'*Always* looking for you, lad. I spend days looking for you. You're never around when you're needed. Where have you been?'

'Sorry, sir. I just heard you'd got a man found dead in bed … with a pig,' he said with a smile. 'In a nightie.'

Angel glared at him. 'A lot's happened since then.'

Crisp could see he wasn't earning any merit marks. 'I got a tip-off that Harry Savage had been seen on a platform at Bromersley railway station,' he said quickly. 'I had to follow it up.'

Harry Savage was a confidence trickster, a particularly cruel kind who had tricked an elderly lady out of £8,000 savings with an insurance scam. He had subsequently been caught but had escaped from the Magistrates' Court at Shiptonthorpe in 2006.

Angel's eyebrows shot up. 'Did you catch him?'

'No, sir.'

'What else have you been busy with?' Angel said.

'Well, then I got a complaint from a woman about noise in Newberry Flats … the flat next to hers. It turned out to be the sound of a cuckoo clock he had just bought. It was on the adjoining wall.'

Angel's knuckles tightened. 'A cuckoo clock?' he bawled. 'Are you wasting police time listening out for cuckoo clocks?'

'Well, it was very loud through those cardboard walls. It was annoying, every hour.'

Angel rubbed his chin. He must hold on to his self-control.

Crisp said: 'Just serving the public, sir. Doing what I can.'

Angel ran his hand through his hair. 'Well, there's something else here you can do to serve the public. There's a Vincent Doonan, desperately ill from gunshot wounds in the General Hospital. Get over there. When he comes round, ask him who shot him. Get what you can from the man. All right?'

Crisp's face straightened.

'If he tells you, phone it through to me immediately.'

'Yes, sir.'

'If he dies, phone *that* through to me immediately, also.'

'Right, sir.'

He went out.

Angel was only seconds behind him. He closed the office door, crossed the corridor and leaned into the CID room. There were a dozen or more policemen and women working at computers or talking to each other. He saw DS Gawber at his desk, frowning and hunched up, having an earnest discussion with somebody on the phone. It looked as if he might be engaged for some time.

Ahmed was at his desk by the door. He saw Angel and stood up. 'Are you wanting something, sir?'

'Oh. Yes. A man was shot last night. I want to know where he lives and if he has any family. Nobody knows his next of kin. His name is Vincent Doonan. You can find out from the electoral roll. A witness thought he lived on Edward Street, but he doesn't know what number. Can I leave that with you? I need to know it ASAP.'

'Right, sir.'

'I'm going down to the Fisherman's Rest on Canal Road. When Ron Gawber is off the phone, ask him to join me there, will you?'

Angel dashed down the corridor, past the cells, to his car.

When he pulled up outside the Fisherman's Rest, one of the SOCO team in white overall suit, hat and Wellington boots was loading plastic bags into their transit van at the door.

Angel went inside.

DS Donald Taylor was removing the white paper overalls over a navy blue suit and changing his shoes. Two other members of SOCO's team were packing plastic 'EVIDENCE' bags into white plastic boxes. At a table, in the customer side of the bar, Clem Bailey was sitting at a table with a coffee pot and dirty beakers in front of him. He was smoking a cigarette. He looked weary and needed a shave.

Taylor threw up a salute.

Angel acknowledged it and pointed with a thumb towards the man. 'Is this Mr Bailey, the landlord, Don?'

'Yes, sir,' Taylor said.

Angel looked across at him. 'I'm DI Angel. Good morning, Mr Bailey. I'd like a few words.'

Bailey took a drag on the cigarette and nodded. 'I'm not going anywhere.'

'You finished here, Don?' Angel said.

'Just about,' Taylor said.

Angel then moved closely up to Taylor and, with his back to Bailey, he looked closely into the sergeant's eyes. 'Anything interesting?' he whispered pointedly.

Taylor shook his head. 'We've got the four glasses bearing the witnesses' and victim's fingerprints, and blood samples from the table … that's all there was. The gunman apparently didn't touch anything and he wore gloves. There were no footprints.'

Angel wrinkled his nose.

'Yes. Right, Don.'

He turned away from Taylor and walked the few steps towards Clem Bailey. 'Do you mind if I sit down?'

Bailey gave a slight shrug and said, 'I've told your chaps all I know.'

'Bear with me, Clem,' he said rubbing his hand across his face. 'Will you take me through what actually happened?'

It took Bailey only a minute to talk and show Angel exactly what happened, then they both returned to chairs by the table.

Angel thought a moment then said, 'Did you know the man who shot Vincent Doonan?'

'No, but I recognized his eyes. Seen them somewhere before. They were mean.'

'So you remember his face?'

Bailey licked his lips. 'I can't put a *name* to him.'

'All right, but would you say that that man knew exactly what he was going to do?'

Bailey looked up. He was surprised. He hadn't been asked a question which required his opinion. 'Yes. Yes, I do. He didn't want a sandwich at all.'

'That was to get you out of the way.'

Bailey nodded.

'So he was afraid you might recognize him.'

'I suppose so.'

'No suppose about it. Why else would he order a sandwich he had no intention of eating, but to get you out of the way?'

'But he ordered a pint.'

'He had to do that to appear normal. But he had been in here before. He *knew* you would have to go into the back to make the sandwich, didn't he?'

Bailey blinked. 'Well, yes.'

Angel nodded and rubbed his mouth. 'What was his voice like?'

'Um, ordinary.'

'Was it strong and aggressive or was it … weak and apologetic or was it something else?'

'It was strong.'

Angel sniffed and said: 'I think you know this man, Clem.'

'I don't. I've no idea who he was.'

'Close your eyes a minute for me. See if you can remember his eyes. You might. He was a strong character. The rest of his face was covered, so you would naturally be inclined to look more closely at the area *not* covered.'

Bailey closed his eyes but he wasn't happy about it.

‘Now then,’ Angel said. ‘What were his eyes like? Were they shiny, or dull?’

‘Shiny. And black.’

‘Black, good. Were the white areas … very white?’

‘No. A dirty grey.’

‘What about his eyebrows? What colour were they? Were they thick?’

‘Thick, and black.’

‘Brown black, grey black or jet black?’

‘Jet black,’ Bailey said, then he opened his eyes and blinked several times. ‘There’s nothing else. If I have my eyes closed any longer, I shall be asleep.’

‘Can you hold that picture in your memory? It’s vitally important. We’re on the hunt for a gunman who might be a murderer.’

The front door banged.

Angel looked round, and when he saw who it was, his face brightened. ‘Excuse me,’ he said to Bailey. ‘I won’t be a minute.’

He stood up and crossed the floor.

‘I found out about the nightdress, sir,’ Gawber said quietly. ‘Pure silk. Got the assistant who actually served Santana. Lucky, that. She said that I wasn’t the first person to be inquiring about Mr Santana’s purchase. She said she thought that Mrs Santana must have been very pleased, and that he wasn’t at all fussy about the colour, but that he wanted it to be silk, roomy and sleeveless.’

Angel said: ‘Confirmation he bought the thing.’

‘Where does that get us, sir?’ Gawber said.

‘Damned if I know.’

Then out of his pocket Angel pulled the scrap of paper Scrivens had given him. He gave it to Gawber.

‘Here, Ron. These are the names and addresses of the three witnesses who were seated with Doonan. Call on them. See what you can find out.’

Gawber took the list, glanced at it and rushed off.

DS Taylor stuck his head through the door. 'We've finished here, sir, and we're all packed up. We're off back up to Tunistone.'

Angel acknowledged him with a wave of the hand. He turned back to Bailey. 'Still holding that picture of the gunman's face,' he said, 'I want you to come back to the station and look at our rogues' gallery, see if you can pick him out.'

Bailey looked pained. 'I won't be able to do that. I haven't seen my bed for nigh on twenty-four hours.'

'It won't take long. I'll take you up and I'll bring you back here. Won't take long, I promise.'

Bailey yawned then shrugged. 'If it'll help.'

Angel nodded, pulled out his mobile and phoned Ahmed.

'I've got an address for Vincent Doonan, sir,' Ahmed said.

'Good. Hang on to it. Got another urgent job for you, lad. I want you to set up a laptop of our head and shoulders rogues' gallery photos, showing only the area of the face from two inches above the eyebrows down to just below the nose, and blanking off the ears. Can you do that quickly and set the laptop up in my office?'

'Yes, sir.'

'I'll be there in ten minutes.'

He closed the phone, but it rang immediately. He reopened it and pressed the talk button. It was Crisp. 'Yes?'

'I'm at the hospital, sir.'

Angel frowned. 'Aye,' he said. 'Go on.' He steeled himself for what he thought was to follow.

'I managed to get to Vincent Doonan, sir,' Crisp said. 'I asked him … I had to ask him several times … who had shot him and he eventually … simply said, "It was Liam Quigley" … and then he died.'

Angel identified a tremor in Crisp's voice. Angel blew out a long breath, then said, 'Right, lad. Come back to the station. I'll meet you there.'

He slowly closed the phone and slipped it back into his pocket.

He remembered the man called Liam Quigley. A big, ugly lump of a man, a small-time crook mostly involved in stealing and selling stolen property in public houses and flea markets. Murder was a big step for him. Angel sighed as he considered how many small-time crooks graduated into committing the worst crime of all. He looked up at Bailey and said, 'It's a case of murder now, Clem.'

Bailey's mouth tightened. The tragic news made him more than willing to look at the rogues' gallery. 'All right then, let's go.'

They both stood up to leave, just as the whirring sound from the mechanism of the cuckoo clock on the wall behind him began its hourly cycle and vulgarly proclaimed that the time was ten o'clock.

Angel looked round at it and frowned.

Ten minutes later, Angel and Bailey were coming down the station corridor as Ahmed was coming up it.

Ahmed said: 'The laptop's ready on your desk, sir.'

'Right,' Angel said and he ushered Bailey into his office.

The two men were soon seated in front of the laptop screen.

Angel expected Liam Quigley to be among the selection of pictures but he couldn't be certain. Quigley had not been in trouble for several years. It was possible his picture had been removed. Altogether, at that moment, there were 108 faces registered, six to a page. Parts of all the faces had been duly blanked off as Angel had instructed. There were no names under the photographs, just numbers.

Bailey began eagerly studying the photographs closely but, not seeing the one he could identify among the early ones, he soon became less intense and clicked the mouse to move on to the next page at his own pace.

Angel watched him as he clicked on page after page. He himself only recognized a few of the villains from their eyes and noses; it wasn't easy, but he had high hopes.

The page with the photograph of Liam Quigley eventually came up. Angel recognized it: the big head was, he thought, a positive giveaway. The photograph had the figure '92' neatly printed in the middle in black underneath. He waited like an excited child on a Christmas morning for Bailey to pick it out.

But he didn't.

Bailey clicked the mouse to move on to the next page, and Angel didn't so much as blink.

Bailey clicked on to the end and then back to the beginning.

He turned to Angel and said, 'No, Mr Angel, he's not there.'

Angel sighed. There was no hiding his disappointment. He stood up. 'Go through them again, in your own time, Clem, will you? This is very important. I've a little job I want to do. I won't be a minute.'

Bailey wasn't pleased, but he turned back to the screen and reached out for the mouse.

Angel went out of the office and closed the door. He crossed the corridor to the CID office and peered through the door. It was unusually quiet. There were two detectives arguing about something at the far end of the room, and Ahmed at his desk by the door. He saw him, stood up and said, 'Looking for me, sir? I want to tell you about Vincent Doonan. I got his address.'

'Ah, yes?'

'He lived on his own at 11 Edward Street.'

'Right, lad. I've got it. Thank you, but right now I'm looking for DS Crisp.'

He looked round. 'He's been in, sir. Not long since. Probably in the canteen.'

'Right, I'll find him. Take two teas into my office, will you? I've left Clem Bailey still looking at the rogues' gallery. There's one for him.'

Ahmed nodded.

Angel went further down the green corridor and pushed his way through the swing doors into the canteen.

He found Crisp on his own at the far end. There was an empty cup and saucer in front of him and his nose was buried in a newspaper.

'Are you all right, lad?' Angel said.

Crisp looked up. He blinked. It was unusual to see Angel in the canteen. 'Oh? Yes, sir.'

Angel dropped into the seat opposite him.

Crisp smiled. 'You're in the papers again, sir.' He pointed to a headline on an inside page and read it out. 'Murdered millionaire in bed with pig in nightie. Super sleuth Angel investigates.'

Angel pulled an angry face and swiped out at the paper, hitting it with his fingertips. 'I wish that rag would get its facts right.'

Crisp grinned.

'I want you to find Liam Quigley and bring him in for questioning. Be careful. He could be armed. Take somebody with you.'

'Right, sir. Where will I find him?'

Angel's fists tightened. 'I thought you were a detective?'

Crisp frowned.

Angel glared at him, then stood up. 'I should try the PNC. If that doesn't help, I should try Confused dot com.'

Crisp shook his head.

Angel returned to his office.

Bailey was drinking the tea.

'I've found him,' Bailey said brightly, putting down the cup. 'Thanks for the tea.'

Angel's face brightened. Good. Good.'

'I've found the man.'

Bailey clicked the mouse a few times, found the page and said, 'There, that's the one there, number twenty.'

Angel stared at the photograph and wrinkled his nose.

CHAPTER 4

Angel drove the BMW through the converted farmhouse gates and saw DS Taylor and a PC both in white boiler suits, rubber boots and caps poking around the modern double garage built at the side.

He stopped the BMW behind SOCO's van, which in turn was behind Santana's silver Mercedes, still parked at the front door.

Taylor saw him, came out of the garage and crossed the drive to greet him.

Angel nodded towards the garage as he got out of the car and said, 'Anything in there?'

'Just a can of petrol, sir. Nothing else.'

'Petrol?' Angel said, rubbing his chin. 'Not diesel?'

'It's definitely petrol. No petrol stations up here. I suppose it's an emergency stock in case they find themselves stuck here with an empty tank.'

Angel frowned.

'Personally I wouldn't like to be stuck here *any time,*' Taylor added. 'It's so … so quiet.'

Angel smiled. He thought he might like it, in small doses. 'That's the beauty of the place,' he said.

Taylor looked up at the black cloudy sky over the distant mountains. 'And it's so eerie.'

They arrived at Santana's car. The door handles, boot catch and the area round the cover of the fuel-tank cap were covered with silver aluminium powder.

Angel nodded towards the car and said, 'It's already been dusted?'

'The outside was done before we broke off to go to the Doonan job, sir.'

'Is it locked?'

Taylor shrugged.

Angel gripped the handle of the driver's door and pulled. It opened. His eyebrows shot up. He looked at Taylor.

'That's how it was, sir.'

Taylor walked round the car and tried the other doors. They were also unlocked.

Angel nodded and peered inside the car. It was clean and tidy and there was nothing untoward. He closed the door.

'You'll dust the steering wheel, handbrake and gear stick?'

'Yes, of course, sir.'

He went round to the boot and opened it. It was big and empty, but around the catch where the lock fitted he saw several strands of an off-white textile. It was much thicker than traditional cotton thread. Angel crouched down to peer at it, but didn't touch it.

Taylor went to the SOCO van behind them and returned with a holdall. He took out a pair of white plastic disposable tweezers in a hermetically sealed bag. He unravelled the strands of thread and carefully inserted them in an 'EVIDENCE' bag.

'Take a swab of the floor of the boot,' Angel said. 'I believe that that pig was transported here via this car. I want that determined, if it's possible.'

'Right, sir. You think somebody else might have brought it here?'

'No, but it's pretty heavy for Santana to have been able to manage on his own.'

Taylor nodded his agreement.

Angel closed the car boot, noted that the model was the S320 cdi, reflected briefly on how much it must have cost and went inside the house. Taylor followed.

The plastic trail of floor covering had now been removed and Angel looked down at the polished parquet floor in the hall and along to the bedroom. 'Did you retrieve any footprints or marks from here?'

'There were lots of shuffle marks but nothing we could use. There was a mark about an inch wide on the floor, rubbing off the polish … couldn't make out what it was. It was in a more or less direct line from the front door to the bedroom door.'

'Was it the pig?'

Taylor's mouth dropped open. 'Could possibly have been the pig … You mean being dragged along?'

Angel nodded as he opened the bedroom door.

The body of Peter Santana had been removed. There was a big ruddy-brown stain where it had been. There were blood spatters on the pretty wallpaper by the door opening and on the white paintwork.

'The shooting must have taken place here, by the door,' Angel said, thinking aloud.

Taylor nodded.

'The body was found fully clothed on the floor just inside the door. He put up a gallant fight before he was shot. Maybe he was defending the pig. It was in that bed, covered over.'

'Defending a dead pig, sir?'

'I mean trying to hide the fact that he had a dead pig in his bed. It could have been an … embarrassment?'

Angel rubbed his chin a while then looked across at Taylor. 'Where was the wrapping from the nightdress?'

'In a wastepaper basket by the dressing table, sir.'

Angel meandered further into the big room. He spotted the empty wastepaper basket.

'Was there anything else in it?'

'No.'

Angel came back towards the bed where the pig had been. Clearly it had been removed and the bed remade.

He stared at the Laura Ashley bedspread then turned to Taylor. 'Have you ever tried to put clothes on to somebody or something unconscious, or inanimate, Don?'

'Can't say that I have.'

'It isn't easy.'

'Do you think that more than one person put that nightdress on the pig, sir?'

'I really don't know,' Angel said. 'I really don't know.'

He caught sight of the silver candelabra with the pink candle wax hanging off the three holders, and he remembered how cold he had been when he had first entered that room earlier in the day. It was still very cold. He turned to Taylor. 'Is there no heating on?'

'I wanted you to see this, sir,' Taylor said, directing him to the hall. 'If you've finished in here.'

He'd finished there for the time being, but he wasn't happy. He gave the room a last look round. This was not promising to be an easy case. His pulse was steady, his eyes slightly narrowed as if in pain, his mind like a box of assorted cogs, each trying to find another to mesh into smoothly, and failing at every attempt.

They left the bedroom and returned to the hall.

Angel noticed a large clock on the wall. It showed the time at eight minutes past twelve. He looked at his watch and found the correct time to be 1.15 exactly.

'The clock's wrong.'

Taylor looked up at him.

Angel put his ear to the face of the mechanism for a few moments. Then he went down on his knee and found a wire feeding out from the back of the clock to an electric socket. It was a very fine antique reproduction clock run from mains electricity.

'The power must have been switched off at eight minutes past twelve. That would be midnight, last night?' Angel said.

'Looks like that, sir,' Taylor said, then he pointed to a table against the wall. On it were four electric fuses. Above the table was a fuse box screwed on to the wood panelling on the wall; it had a door on the front of it, which was partly open. Inside was a line of a dozen fuses and spaces for the four fuses on the table below.

'That's why it is cold everywhere, sir,' Taylor said. 'Those fuses put half the house in darkness and knocked off the central heating. We've checked them for fingerprints and they've been wiped clean.'

Angel raised his eyebrows slightly.

'Wiped clean?'

'Yes, sir. The murderer must have come in the front door,' Taylor said, 'pulled the fuses, wiped them clean of his prints. That would put the place in darkness. That's why Santana was using the candles.'

'That means the murderer must have been in the house ... hiding, while Santana found the candelabra and lit it. And Santana would have had to pass the fuse box to get it from the dining room. Also the intruder would have been wiping the fuses in the dark. I don't think so.'

'Maybe he had a torch?'

'He'd need three hands then. He'd have to put the torch down, and anyway, the light would have told Santana of his presence. Have the fuses been photographed?'

'Yes, sir.'

'Is there a fault?'

'Don't know. With your permission, sir, I'll put the fuses in now and ... see what happens.'

Angel nodded. He turned back to Taylor. 'Why would they be wiped clean?'

Taylor busied himself pressing the fuses into their respective holders.

The lights came on, and the hum of some sort of machine from the pool room started behind them. They crossed the hall and looked through the glass at the turquoise water.

Angel opened the door and went in. The hum was louder.

'A water pump, I expect.'

Chlorine in the air made Angel wrinkle his nose.

The big, inviting-looking swimming pool was screened by large windows on two sides. He saw that they looked out on to heather-covered mountains and a grey cloudy sky. At the far end of the room on a tiled area was a massage table and four body-building machines. He looked at them enviously and thought that they would have provided a thorough workout for the most ardent bodybuilder.

Angel came out of the pool room and closed the door. He turned to Taylor and said, 'Check if the appliances or lights extinguished by pulling those four fuses are in safe working order. There must have been some reason for the murderer putting half the place in darkness. And by the way, whose prints were on the candelabra?'

'Santana's, sir. Clear and distinct.'

'Hmmm. And there were no signs of an intruder breaking in?'

'There were no signs of anyone breaking into the house *anywhere*, sir. The front door was closed but not locked. It surprised the housekeeper. She said that Mr Santana was usually so careful, and he was a creature of habit.' Angel nodded. He knew what that meant. He was a creature of habit himself. His mobile began to ring. He fished into his pocket and pulled it out.

It was Crisp. 'Liam Quigley lives at 24 Sebastopol Terrace, sir. I'm standing on his doorstep. I've been knocking on the door for the past ten minutes. There's no sign of life. Of course, he might be out. What shall I do?'

Angel's lips tightened back against his teeth. 'Don't mess about, lad. Get a warrant for his arrest. He's been identified as the murderer of Vincent Doonan, hasn't he? It was *your* ear Doonan whispered his name into, wasn't it?'

'Yes, sir.'

'Well, Quigley might be dodging us. Get a warrant to search his house. Then get in there. If he's there, bring him in, and look sharp about it.'

He closed the phone with a click, blew out a foot of air and stuffed the mobile back into his pocket.

He turned back to Taylor and said, 'What else is there to see?'

Together, they visited the other rooms in the house. Angel had a general trudge round. He saw nothing remarkable in any of them. He checked on the windows, which were all closed, locked and secure.

It was becoming clear that the murderer must have entered the house by the front door, that he knew his way around the house and had therefore been well known to Peter Santana. It must have been somebody who would benefit from his death. As Santana was enormously rich, a motive shouldn't be difficult to find. He ruminated on these matters as he returned silently to the hall and up to the front door.

He thanked Taylor and went outside. It was now quite gloomy and in the cold air he could see that fog was not far away. He walked all around the lonely house. There were no trees on the moors, the strong winds had seen to that, but there was a good stone wall around the house. He trudged up the drive looking in every direction. He went through the open gates, which appeared to be left permanently open. He peered round the stone pillars from which they were hung. At the base of one of the pillars he saw several recently snapped twigs of dormant gorse. He wandered further around the area, across more gorse, some heather and grass, but found no other signs of disturbance. He pursed his lips and, standing in the cold, considered the explanation. Someone had been standing there, very recently … could have had binoculars and been watching the house. He crouched down hopeful that the snooper might have dropped something or left a heel mark or something. But there was nothing.

He returned to his car.

It was only a ten-minute drive to the police station, and Angel spent most of the time thinking about the murder of Peter Santana. It was such an unusual and disconcerting case.

The newspapers were having a great time, with headlines such as, 'The pig and the producer', 'Hamming it up', 'How millionaire brought home the bacon', and so on. Angel knew he ought to be in and among the people associated with Santana to find out what had made him tick, but they would have to wait. There were more pressing matters. He had a lot on his mind.

He walked quickly down the green-painted station corridor to his office, picked up the phone and tapped out a number. Ahmed answered.

'There was a villain picked out by Clem Bailey yesterday from our rogues' gallery, Ahmed. Number twenty,' he said while unbuttoning his raincoat.

'Yes, sir. I looked it up. That was Laurence Smith.'

Angel's eyebrows shot up. 'Laurence Smith? Larry the Liar?'

'I don't know about that, sir.'

'Well, get out all you can on him for me, pronto.'

'Right, sir.'

Angel knew Laurence Smith, a difficult man who had the reputation of being an habitual liar. He had served time for robbery and dealing in stolen goods.

Angel peeled off the raincoat threw it over a chair and looked down at his desk. At the top of a pile of post and reports was an email from the Drugs and Abusive Substances Squad, London. It was addressed to senior officers at each of the forty-three police forces in the UK.

The following paragraph caught his attention:

As a result of stringent searching and recent arrests of smugglers concealing heroin inside children's teddy bears and 50 kilo sacks of dried currants, smugglers have turned to concealing the drug in hollow plastic rolling pins in children's toy baking sets, hollow wooden children's toy forts and other unusual wooden and mechanical toys, ornaments and household equipment. All officers are asked to be aware of the devious methods and unusual containers smugglers have been driven to concealing the drug and the Drug and Abusive Substances Squad request your cooperation.

As he was re-reading the email, the phone rang. He reached out for it.

'Angel,' he growled.

'Crisp here, sir. Got the warrant. Got a squad of four men together at the front of the station to mount that raid on Quigley's pad. Just filling up with diesel. Will be leaving in two minutes.'

'Right. I'll follow you in my car.'

The two cars glided quietly up to the front door of Quigley's terraced house in the Canal Road area of Bromersley. There was a light showing through thick curtains drawn across the downstairs front room. Two constables moved swiftly through the ginnel to the back of the house, while Angel, Crisp and a constable with a battering ram approached the front door.

Crisp began to bang loudly on the door. 'Police, Quigley. Open up. It's the police. Come on, Quigley. Open up. Open up.'

Angel rubbed his cold hands together to try to warm them up, while the constable and Crisp maintained the racket at the front door. Then Crisp gave the signal and the constable let heave with the battering ram and the door flew open.

They rushed out of the cold into the front room, but there was nobody there. They dispersed rapidly throughout the little house, switching on all the lights. The men covering the back door rushed back down the ginnel and into the house through the front door. Every room was checked but nobody was found.

Crisp was last down the stairs. 'He's not here, sir.'

They all congregated in the kitchen.

Angel looked round the tiny room. It was clean and tidy. There were no pots in the sink; everything was washed up.

Suddenly they heard the whirring sound from the mechanism of the cuckoo clock on the wall beginning its hourly cycle.

Angel recognized the noise, turned round and stared at it. He rubbed his chin. He looked closely at the weights to note which weight fell as the cuckoo proclaimed that the time was five o'clock. It was the weight on the shortest length of chain, an inch or so from the underside of the clock. The other weight was almost at the floor. From that he knew that the clock had only recently been wound up.

He said nothing. They had searched the place and Quigley wasn't there. He ran his hand through his hair. He turned round and realized also that the room was warm. He saw a radiator on the kitchen wall covered with a towel. He put his hand on it and found that it was damp. Then he spotted an electric kettle. He patted it carefully. It was warm. The muscles in his jaw tightened.

He *knew* that Quigley was there.

Angel, Crisp and the constables searched the ground floor again. There was no cellar, just a hallway, two rooms and a pantry. Then they went upstairs and carefully looked through the two bedrooms and the bathroom. Angel even opened the cistern cupboard. There was not so much as a hungry spider.

The squad gathered on the small landing. Angel signalled to one of the constables, who leaned across to him; he whispered something in his ear. The man immediately went downstairs and returned with a long-handled sweeping brush, which he silently handed to him. Angel took it and pointed it up to the ceiling and pressed it against the wooden trapdoor that led to the loft. He pushed but it did not give. He tried in several other positions, but with the same result.

'He's up there,' Angel said at length. 'He's either holding the door down or he's put some weight on top of it.'

'How did he get up there?' Crisp said.

'Got a ladder and pulled it up behind him, I expect,' Angel said.

'What can we do, sir?'

Angel pointed downstairs and put his first finger vertically across his lips.

The squad made their way downstairs to the kitchen.

'He may be able to hear all we are saying.' He turned to the constable who had driven the van. 'Nip back to the station to the stores and bring back some steps or a ladder, sharpish.'

'Right, sir,' he said and he was gone.

'He may have planned this way of escape and could have victuals and supplies up there to last for days,' Angel said.

The men waited patiently in the kitchen. Angel looked at his watch. He pulled out a chair, sat down, picked up his mobile and tapped in his home number.

'Hello, love. Are you all right?'

'Where are you?' Mary said. 'You're not ringing to say you're going to be late again, are you?'

'Something came up. I might be an hour or two. Anything in the post?'

Her voice went up an octave. 'An hour or two? And I've made a beef casserole with onion and kidney and mushroom. It's been slow cooking for three hours. I timed it for six o'clock. After that it will start drying up. What am I supposed to do about it, Michael? Tell me that.'

'I'm sorry, love. It's unavoidable.'

Angel noticed that Crisp was smiling down at him. He looked away.

Angel's fingers tightened round the phone. 'Put it on a low light,' he said, 'and I'll get back as soon as I can.'

'It'll dry up. It's too bad, it really is.'

'Is there anything in the post?'

Her voice lightened. 'As a matter of fact there is. We've got a wedding invitation. Who do you think is getting married?'

The guessing business always rattled him. 'I don't know, do I?' he growled.

'Don't be so irritable. Why, little Timmy, of course.'

The pupils of his eyes made a quick sweep of their sockets. He licked his lip quickly then said, 'Who is little Timmy then?'

'My godson, Timothy, of course.'

Angel frowned and shook his head. 'I don't know any Timothy.'

'My sister-in-law's cousin's youngest boy, Timothy Joseph Stolworthy. Of course you do.'

He remembered. 'Oh, him!'

He remembered him as a baby, and that it cost Mary £25 every Christmas and every spring, for the little monster's birthday, and he never replied, never phoned and they never ever saw him. Mary used to pay it out gracefully. Angel had said it was like throwing money down a black hole.

'Such a nice little boy.'

'I have never seen him,' he said.

'You saw him at Grace's wedding,' she snapped.

He didn't remember. He didn't want to argue, and he couldn't have cared less. 'Right. Well, where do they live these days?'

'Cornwall. They've always lived in Cornwall.'

'Well, we can't go down to Cornwall,' he said.

'The wedding's in Las Vegas.'

'*Las Vegas*!' he bawled. 'We'll talk about this later.'

'We'll have to buy them a present.'

He wrinkled his nose. 'Send them money.'

'Can't send *money* for a wedding present.'

He had had enough of this irritating and potentially expensive chatter. He was relieved when he heard some noise in the next room. Crisp and some others dashed out of the room.

'Duty calls, love. Got to go. Goodbye.' He closed the phone with a snap and thrust it back in his pocket.

The squad driver had returned with a ladder, which he quietly manipulated up the stairs with difficulty and eventually rested against the trapdoor over the landing. The squad followed him upstairs. The constable with the battering ram went up the ladder first and removed the door with surprising ease. He pushed the door cover to one side and came down the steps.

Angel took up the position on the ladder. He took his powerful torch with him, put his head through the hole and shone the flashlight around the cobwebby beams, slates and brickwork. The beam caught a big man in his underpants and vest crouching down in front of a roughly cemented redbrick-built chimney stack at the far end of the dusty space. He was attempting the impossible. He was desperately trying to hide in a place where there was no cover.

'Come on out, Quigley,' Angel said. 'You're copped.'

CHAPTER 5

An hour later, Angel re-read the report he had just finished on the day's events, pulled a face at it, and yawned as he rammed it in the desk drawer. He glanced at his watch, put on his coat, came out of the office and was met by Crisp coming up from the direction of the cells.

'He's been checked by the MO, sir. I've got his clothes organized. He's had some fish and chips and two mugs of tea. And a KitKat.'

Angel shook his head. 'And are you going to offer to read him a bedtime story?'

Crisp's eyes flashed.

Angel glared at him and said, 'Does Quigley know that his solicitor, Bloomfield, is coming to see him any time now, and does Bloomfield understand that his client will be formally interviewed at nine o'clock tomorrow morning?'

'Not yet, sir. No.'

'Well, *tell* him, lad. *Tell* him. And have you left a note and the warrant for Don Taylor requesting SOCO to search Quigley's house ASAP tomorrow?'

'Not yet, sir. No.'

Angel sighed. 'Well, *do* it, lad. Do it now. And do you know where you have to be at 8.28 in the morning?'

'No, sir.'

'In my office.'

Crisp's jaw dropped.

'Any questions?' Angel said.

'No.'

'Right. Then I bid you good night.'

Angel went down the corridor, past the cells and out through the back door. It was getting quite cold. He drove out of the police car park, through the town centre. He saw a brightly illuminated fish and chip shop as he stood at traffic lights. The smell of vinegar dribbling over hot batter sneaked through the car ventilation system. The bouquet was more seductive than Chanel to a weary copper on a freezing cold December night. There were only two customers at the counter, and he didn't really fancy warmed-up stew and cabbage.

'Good morning, sir.'

'Good morning, lad. Come in. Sit down. Now, about Felicity Santana.'

'Yes, sir. Felicity Santana. She's rated as being in the top ten most glamorous women in the world. I'd personally put her in the top three.'

'Thereby is the problem,' Angel said with a sniff. 'Even with your way with the ladies, I don't think you could get anywhere near her.'

Crisp was not pleased but he managed a controlled smile.

Angel added: 'There would be intense competition from some of the film world's leading men … with bulging wallets, and fast cars, and with diamond bracelets and giant solitaire rings dripping from their pockets.'

'I'd enjoy giving it a go, sir.'

'I expect you would. And then there's her entourage of fans, managers, make-up, hairdo and beauty wallahs and so on.'

Crisp still looked at Angel across the desk with a confident smile. 'I'd be willing to try, sir.'

Angel shook his head. 'Just think about this, lad. The problem is that it is almost certain that she had something to do with her husband's death. The marriage didn't seem to be much. The age difference. His health. His total attachment to his business, his stories and his films. Even when she returned home late at night, she didn't hesitate to admit to me that she didn't look in his room to see if he was awake to say hello, or good night, or to see if he was all right.'

'I thought she was in the studio at the time of his murder?'

'I don't think so,' he said. 'At this stage, I don't know, but you are moving away from the plan.'

Crisp looked up. 'Oh? A plan, sir?'

'There's always a plan. Can't work without a plan.'

Crisp's face brightened.

Angel said: 'In any group of people, any gathering, any assembly, any team, there's always one sad little person who works hard, is full of enthusiasm but is never appreciated. They're always at the bottom of the pile ... always being walked on.'

'Yes, sir. That's me.'

Angel's eyes flashed and he glared across the desk at him. 'I am not talking about *you*, lad,' he bawled. 'It *isn't* you. And I'm *not* talking about *here*. I'm talking about the likely situation at the Top Hat film company. I'm referring to Felicity Santana's personal gofer, or whatever they're called.'

Crisp frowned. 'Oh? What's she like, sir? And what's her name?'

'I don't know. That's for you to find out. I don't even know if it is a girl. Boys often do the job.'

Crisp's jaw dropped. 'But, sir. I can't make up to a boy.'

'That'll be the one who sees everything, knows what's going on, has nobody to confide in because nobody notices him or her. A bit of appreciation and they'll happily cooperate. You know what I want?'

'You want the dirt on Felicity Santana.'

'You don't have to be so crude,' he said and sighed.

Crisp stifled a smile.

'The situation clearly is this. Felicity Santana is a very beautiful woman. We know that she picked out Peter Santana ten years ago and got him to marry her. We know he was a tough nut. So he presumably knew what he was letting himself in for. That also shows that she must be a shrewd operator too. Anyway, I believe that after ten years, she thought that Peter Santana was lasting too long. Maybe she had plenty of money in her purse, but she never got the time to spend it. She never had any time to play. She wanted out of the marriage, so she started looking around and met another sucker and set up a deal. Made promises to some money-grabbing male with a big enough ego that if he disposed of Peter Santana for her, that would secure his rights to the key to her bedroom, a pretty lump of her lovely millions and a share in whatever she earned in the future. They shook hands on it, and the deed was done. Santana was murdered. She may even have helped the new man. Anyway, when her husband took his last breath, she became a very *rich*, beautiful woman, who has a pile of money as high as Strangeways tower. There's also a man somewhere who has won the right to put a ring on her finger and everything else that goes with it. Any questions so far?'

'No, sir.'

'We don't yet know who he is. It isn't him we have to watch. She'll have been super selective. Remember, she could have had the pick of the field. But she will have tended to seduce someone she knew *well* ... *very* well. The last ten years Santana worked her so hard that her range of suckers must be among the men she worked with. There was no time or opportunity to develop a relationship among the Hollywood set, or even here in the film-producing belt in the home counties. I believe it has to be here in her husband's own business, here, at Top Hat. All right?'

Crisp nodded.

'I have prepared a list of characteristics that would fit the man she might have made such a pact with. He would be dishonest, ruthless, handsome, rich and probably older than her. Write them down. They are tremendously important. Find the man with those attributes and you've found the murderer.'

'That's a profile, sir,' Crisp said.

'Call it what you like. Just find the man that it fits. That's your brief.'

'You make it sound simple, sir.'

'It is simple. What *I'd* do is apply for a job at the studio, see what happens. It's a start. It would get you through the gates. From then on I'd play it by ear.'

Crisp looked as if he'd bitten on a lemon thinking it was an orange. He was rubbing his cheek.

'You needn't report in until you've got some useful information,' Angel added. 'But don't mess about. We'll contact each other on our mobiles. Leave yours open as long as you can.'

'What do I know about making films?'

Angel looked across at him, shook his head and breathed out a sigh. 'You wouldn't even make a good crook, would you, lad?' He looked at his watch. 'It's nearly nine. Come on. Time for that interview with Quigley. Sit in with me before you go. There's nobody else.'

'Right, sir,' he said.

'And try and look intelligent.'

He switched on the recording machine. 'Interview 9.02 a.m. Thursday 18 December. Present Liam Quigley, Mr Bloomfield, DS Crisp and DI Angel.'

Angel turned to Liam Quigley and said, 'Now then, you've slept on it, lad – what can you tell me about the shooting of Vincent Doonan in the Fisherman's Rest on Tuesday night?'

'Nuttin',' the big Irishman said. 'I told you that last night.'

'And I told you that your name was whispered by Doonan to one of my officers as the one who fired the three shots into him that eventually killed him.'

'I dunno. He must have had a grudge against me.'

'Why? Why would he have a grudge against you?'

'He had a thing going with my daughter.'

'What sort of a thing?'

He hesitated. 'Whenever things got umpty, she used to leave my house to go and stay with him.'

'How old is she?'

'That's not the flaming point,' he roared. 'She was my daughter. She was all I had. We were great pals, and were very close when her mother left. He had no right to … He had no right to entice her away.'

'Where is she now?'

Quigley rubbed his chin. 'I don't know. I wish I did.'

'Got a photograph?'

Quigley reached into his pocket, fished into his wallet and put one postcard-sized photograph on the table. Angel reached out for it. She was a pretty girl with long red hair.

'We'll copy this and return it to you, Mr Quigley. How old is she?'

'Eighteen, but she was only seventeen when this all started. Vincent Doonan was fifty years old. Nearly old enough to be her grandfather. I have been down to his mucky little house more than half a dozen times to bring her back. He hated my guts.'

'When was the last time you went there?'

'Tuesday, except that she wouldn't come back.'

'What happened?'

'She wouldn't come back.'

Angel's fists tightened. 'You said *that*. *Why* wouldn't she come back?'

'It's got nothing to do with it. It needed hardly any daft little ting and she'd take off down to Doonan's. It got to the stage where I could hardly say anything to her. The other day I said that the milk was off, which it was. She took that as a criticism of her management of the catering. It wasn't. She didn't see it like that. She used it as an excuse. And she was off like a loose horse at the Kilkenny races. I have provided well for her, Mr Angel. You've seen my house. She's got a nice room of her own; she needs for nothing.'

'Except perhaps a mother figure.'

'Not my fault the cow went back to Ireland.'

'We shall have to find your daughter … interview her. What's her name?'

'Sonya, but she won't be able to tell you anything. And she's done notting wrong … notting you can touch her for. This is all Doonan's fault. He used to give her ciggies with grass in them. If I found any on her I used to burn them. He was a bad influence all round.'

Angel shook his head. He could have spent all day talking to Quigley about his relationship with his daughter, and her relationship with Vincent Doonan. It didn't promise to prove useful. And Quigley himself was no saint. He'd served time for robbing a Lion Security van outside a bank in Wakefield, as well as a large computer and TV warehouse on a commercial estate in Bromersley. He was also suspected of being involved in other major robberies but as yet nothing could be proved.

Angel was resigned to moving the questioning onwards.

'Where are you employed at the moment?'

'Huh. You know damned well that I haven't a job. You know I couldn't get a job to save my life, and that I'm living on the unemployment money.'

People who sponged off the state always annoyed Angel. 'Seems to me you're living better than I am,' he said.

Bloomfield looked up with a severe face. He stared hard at Angel to catch his attention.

Angel gave a slight shrug, acknowledging that he may have gone a little too far. But he could see that even at a time of high inflation, Quigley's standard of living indicated that money was entering his pocket faster than it was leaving it.

'I'm good with money,' Quigley said. 'Always been able to save. My house is paid for. I don't need a lot to … get around.'

'How much is the insurance on your new Range Rover?'

Quigley's eyes flashed. His head and hands made small rapid movements as if he'd had a charge of electricity through him. 'Don't know.'

'More than your dole money, I'd wager,' Angel said.

'I don't think so.'

'I do. Why did you run away from us and hide in your loft when we knocked on your front door?'

'I knew you were the bogeys and that you were going to run me in for something … something I didn't do.… You always do.… Like this murder you're trying to stick on me.'

'Where were you last Tuesday night at nine o'clock.'

'This is an intrusion of my privacy,' Quigley said and he looked at Bloomfield for support.

There was none coming. Mr Bloomfield shook his head and with a finger indicated that he should answer the question.

Angel also noticed the gesture.

The muscles on Quigley's face tightened. He was an angry man. He looked down.

'Well?' Angel said.

Quigley rubbed his chin several times, then he said, 'I was with a … a friend.'

'Who, and where? From when until what time?'

He wrinkled his nose and didn't look up. 'Her name is Juanita Freedman if you must know. She lives at 11 Bull's Foot Railway Arches on Wath Road. I was with her from about six o'clock in the evening, and I stayed all that night.'

Angel wrote the name and address down. It sounded unlikely. He couldn't imagine who would want him staying with them, especially through the night but in his job, Angel had found that all manner of people made strange bedfellows. Obviously he was going to be speaking with Miss Freedman, and Quigley knew that he would.

Quigley added: 'I don't want that bandying about the place, you know. Technically, I am still married. If my missus got to know, it could cost me a fortune, you understand?'

'Yeah. Yeah,' Angel said. 'Why didn't you tell me this last night?'

Quigley shrugged. 'It's my business. I didn't think it would get this far. You are going to let me go now?'

'If I get satisfactory confirmation of this from … Miss Freedman.'

The interview with Quigley was terminated at 0922 hours. Liam Quigley was taken back to a cell in the station, Mr Bloomfield left immediately, presumably for his office in the town, Crisp left the station to begin his undercover job looking into the background of Felicity Santana, while Angel drove down to 11 Bull's Foot Railway Arches on Wath Road on the outskirts of Bromersley to interview Miss Juanita Freedman.

Number eleven was next to a scruffy little antique shop which was the end shop of a small, busy frontage of shops. It had a large estate agent's 'For Sale' sign secured to the front. At the side of the shop window was a door, which had an illuminated bell-push button on the jamb. Underneath it was a small neat handwritten label that read, 'No 11. Juanita Freedman'. He pressed the button, and as he waited he stepped back and looked into the window of the antique shop next door. He peered closely through the glass and saw a woman in a black dress leaning on the counter reading something. She was surrounded by old pictures, old furniture, old stuff of all kinds. There were no customers in the shop, the shop front needed a fresh coat of paint and the stock seemed dusty. He wondered if the owner had lost interest. He pressed the bell at number eleven again. There was still no reply. He grunted. Miss Freedman was obviously out. He turned and made his way back and past the shop window and through the door. The jingle of a bell on a spring, triggered by the opening of the door, caused the woman to look up from her reading matter. She smiled and fluttered her eyelashes. Angel guessed she was about fifty, desperately trying to look thirty.

'I am looking for Miss Juanita Freedman,' he said. 'I believe she lives in the flat above this shop.'

'I am Juanita Freedman,' she said, raising her eyebrows. 'How can I help you?' She had a pleasant, warm, deep voice.

'DI Angel, Bromersley police, Miss Freedman. I am making inquiries into the whereabouts of Liam Quigley last Tuesday night.'

'Tuesday night?' she gasped. Her eyes flashed then closed. The smile vanished. She put a hand up to cover her face, which flushed up the colour of a judge's robe. 'Oh dear,' she said. 'Oh dear.' After a moment, she took her hand away, opened her eyes, lifted her head and said, 'You *know* already, don't you? He's told you.'

Angel stared at her, trying to look expressionless. 'I beg your pardon,' he said.

'He was with me, Inspector,' she said in a small voice.

Angel nodded. 'He was not out of your sight, the entire evening? I am particularly concerned about the hour, say, between 9 p.m. and 10 p.m.'

'He was here. Every minute. He was concerned about his daughter, Sonya. He was telling me all about her. He came at teatime and left at …' Her voice became almost soundless. She looked at the floor and then added, 'And stayed until about eight o'clock Wednesday morning.'

'Thank you,' Angel said, rubbing his chin.

He wrinkled his nose. He took a sidelong look at Miss Freedman. She wasn't that unattractive. She spoke nicely and sounded well educated. She must have been pretty desperate to want to spend time with Liam Quigley. Angel squeezed the lobe of his ear between finger and thumb. The alibi was something of a setback. He would have to start looking elsewhere for the murderer of Vincent Doonan. Even though Crisp could say on oath that Doonan had told him that it was Quigley who had shot him, there was nothing and nobody else to support the fact. The CPS simply wouldn't have sufficient evidence to make a case strong enough to get a conviction.

After a few moments, in a soft, genteel voice she said, 'Is Mr Quigley in some kind of trouble, Inspector?'

'He might be, Miss Freedman. He might very well be. I am looking into the murder of Vincent Doonan. Do you happen to know anything about it?'

She blinked. Her face changed again. 'Murder?' Her lips moved silently before she added, 'Certainly not.' Her chest heaved several times. 'And I shouldn't expect Mr Quigley to have anything to do with … anything like that either.'

Angel noted her earnestness and nodded in acknowledgement.

She looked relieved and eventually forced a smile.

He glanced round. He liked Victorian and Edwardian furniture and almost everything else he saw in the shop. 'I see the business is for sale?'

'Sadly, yes,' she said. 'The property also.'

Then he heard a short recurring mechanical buzzing sound. It reminded him of the ticking of the detonator of a time bomb he had heard in his training on an explosives course sixteen years ago. It was a noise he had heard several times over the past two or three days. He quickly found the direction from where it came and was looking square on at a cuckoo clock.

The cuckoo showed eleven times.

Angel watched the chiming with interested amusement, then he frowned, turned back to Miss Freedman and said, 'May I suggest that that cuckoo clock is not antique?'

'Indeed it is not, Inspector. It's brand new. The justification for it being on show in the shop is that it is – as we say – a curio.'

'Yes, indeed,' he said and he walked up to the clock. On the wall next to it was a neat handwritten ticket that said: 'Cuckoo Clock £10'.

He frowned again. Ten pounds? He wondered if a nought had maybe dropped off the end of the ticket.

'Ten pounds? Seems a fair price,' he said, to verify the cost.

'I think it's a bargain,' she said.

'I'll take it,' Angel said, pulling out his wallet.

'Thank you, Inspector,' she said brightly. 'I'll get you one in a sealed box.'

She turned away from the counter and opened a door into a room behind her. Angel noticed that it was stacked from the floor to the ceiling with cardboard boxes of the same shape and design. She reached in, picked up the nearest box and returned to the counter.

Angel took a £10 note out of his wallet.

CHAPTER 6

Angel picked up the phone and tapped in a number.

'DS Taylor, SOCO,' a voice answered.

'Angel here. I hope you've finished going over Quigley's drum.'

'Just making out the report, sir. We found nothing incriminating there. You only asked us to search it?'

'And repair the door.'

'That's done.'

'Because I'm releasing him.'

Taylor's voice went up an octave. 'I thought you had evidence, sir?'

'Got an alibi,' Angel said with a sniff. 'Now what about your findings on the Santana place?'

'It's all done, sir. Just needs typing up.'

'Bring your notes down. There are some things I need to know urgently.'

'Right, sir. I'll come down straightaway.'

'Make it ten minutes,' he said and replaced the phone. He went out of the office down to the cells. He asked the duty jailer to let him into Quigley's cell.

When Quigley saw Angel he got to his feet. 'Now what?' he said. 'What new caper are you going to be putting me through?'

'I've spoken to Miss Freedman and ... she confirms your statement. You are free to go.'

'I should frigging well think so.'

Angel led him out of the cell and up to the duty sergeant, where he sulkily collected his possessions and some paperwork was dealt with.

As they walked to the front door of the station, Angel said: 'Do you need transport home?'

Quigley's eyes flashed. 'What? In one of your bloody police cars?'

'Well, you're surely not expecting us to hire a stretch limo for you, are you?'

Quigley glared at him and said: 'I can get a taxi, and pay for it myself.' Then he pushed his way through the glass door and outside to freedom.

Angel watched him go.

Quigley walked quickly to the end of the street then round the corner towards town.

Angel sighed then returned to his office. He found Ahmed waiting at the door. 'What is it, lad? Come in.'

'I've got that stuff on Laurence Smith, sir,' he said, opening a cream file.

'Ah, yes,' Angel said. 'Let's see. Does it say how tall he is?'

Ahmed blinked then delved into the file. 'Six feet, two inches, sir.'

Angel pursed his lips. 'That was the same height as Liam Quigley,' he said, mostly for his own benefit.

Ahmed nodded.

But Angel couldn't remember any other feature that was similar. His hair was a much lighter brown colour for one thing, he recalled. But even so, that wasn't relevant to the ID in this instance: the killer's hair was covered with a woolly hat. He looked up at Ahmed. 'What's Smith's address now?' he said.

'Last known address 36 Sebastopol Terrace, sir.'

'Leave the file with me and ask DI Asquith if he could possibly spare two men to go down there and bring Smith in for questioning.'

'Right, sir,' Ahmed said and dashed off, as DS Taylor came in.

'Ah, Don,' Angel said. 'Sit down.'

'I've brought that report on Quigley's house, sir, just for the record,' Taylor said.

'Leave it there, Don,' he said, pointing to the other file on his desk. 'I'll read it later. Right now, tell me about Peter Santana's Mercedes.'

'There was nothing surprising there, sir. Santana's fingerprints were on the door handle, gear stick, handbrake and steering wheel. They were also on the catch on the boot. I did a swab on the floor area of the boot, and can confirm that the dead pig had been there.'

Angel nodded. It was only what he expected. 'There were some threads or something on the catch where the boot lock is.'

'Yes, sir. They were threads from the cheesecloth that the pig was wrapped in.'

'Ah yes. And the mark on the polished floor of the hall?'

'That was where the pig was dragged into the downstairs bedroom. There were a few tiny pieces of gravel from the drive outside consistent with the pig having been rested in the drive momentarily before it was dragged into the house.'

'And there were no indications to suggest that anyone other than Peter Santana had been in or anywhere near his car the night he was murdered?'

'No, sir.'

'So, we now know that the pig was put in that particular car at the abattoir as the man had said, that Santana drove it up to the lodge and, heavy though it is, he apparently single-handedly dragged it out of the car boot, along the hall, into the bedroom.'

Taylor nodded. 'It's a fair assumption, sir.'

‘Now then.’ He stopped and sighed. ‘Did he put the nightdress on the pig by himself, or did the man who murdered him assist him first?’

Taylor watched a fly flitting round the office window and hoped for inspiration. Angel rubbed his chin.

‘Perhaps we’ll never know,’ Taylor said.

Angel said: ‘Were there any other prints on the fancy cellophane wrapping that the nightdress was wrapped in?’

‘No, sir.’

‘Then it’s a fair assumption that Santana dressed the pig in the nightdress by himself.’

‘Surely the more important question is *why*?’ said Taylor.

Angel nodded. ‘When we know that, we shall know who murdered him.’

‘Well, it’s got me beat, sir,’ said Taylor.

‘At the moment, it’s got me beat, too.’

Taylor smiled. ‘You’ll solve it, sir. This is just your cup of tea, isn’t it?’

There was a compliment in there somewhere. Angel didn’t feel like acknowledging it. He had doubts. He had the reputation of always solving his cases; this might be the one that would spoil that record.

‘We’ll see,’ he muttered.

‘All that we have to deal with now, sir, is Vincent Doonan’s house,’ Taylor said. ‘We should be able to start that tomorrow.’

Angel nodded. ‘As soon as you possibly can.’

‘Of course,’ Taylor said and stood up to go.

‘Just a minute, Don,’ Angel said and he leaned down to the floor and picked up the cardboard box he had brought back from the antique shop and put it on the desk. It was still sealed.

Taylor looked at it and frowned.

Angel said: ‘You will have seen the latest report from the Drugs and Abusive Substances Squad. The one about heroin being found inside children’s toys, hollow wooden toy forts and other wooden objects, ornaments and household paraphernalia.'

'Yes. I've seen it, sir.'

'In here is a cuckoo clock,' Angel said.

Taylor shook his head. 'A cuckoo clock, sir?'

'The town is flooded with them. Everywhere you go, there's one of these on the wall. There's a shop downtown with hundreds in stock. They're pushing them out at a tenner a time.'

Taylor's eyebrows shot up. 'Ten pounds? Cheap enough. Do they work, sir? Do they keep good time?'

'Apparently.'

'Where do they come from? Taiwan? China?'

'Switzerland. I want you to take this one and have a good look at it. See if there are any hollow places where drugs, particularly heroin, are stashed or have been stashed. There must be some reason why there are so many over here, and why they are being peddled so cheaply. And I want you to find out what it is.'

'Right, sir,' Taylor said. 'If there's anything concealed in it, I'll find it.' Then he picked up the box and left.

Angel watched him close the door. He rubbed his chin. He was still wondering and worrying about Peter Santana and the business with the pig. He stood up and walked around the tiny office for a few minutes. His eyes caught sight of the two new files on his desk. He reached out for the one about Laurence Smith, created by Ahmed, extracted from the NPC. He opened it up, sat down and began to read it.

Essentially, it said that Smith had been found guilty with two others in 2001 of stealing 120 yards of copper wire from a stretch of the signalling system than ran alongside the railway line between Bromersley and Wakefield. Smith was awarded six months, which he had served in HMP Lincoln. Interestingly, his two accomplices were Vincent Doonan and Harry Savage. Subsequently, Smith was found guilty on his own in 2002 of robbing a petrol station in Sheffield of £1,200, for which he had served four years in Strangeways.

Angel blew out a length of air noisily. Doonan and Smith had done a job together. That was something of a surprise and maybe a coincidence. Thieves often fall out among themselves. But it confirmed the possibility that Clem Bailey could have made an accurate identification.

Angel knew that Harry Savage was on the run following his dramatic escape from the Magistrates' Court at Shiptonthorpe in March last. He recalled the crime of the stealing of the copper wire, the subsequent offence of conning an old lady out of her £8,000 savings with a fake insurance scam, and there was another unusual job. He stole a load of special paper from a delivery lorry parked outside a transport café on the A1 near Scotch Corner in April. They knew that that job was down to him because he left amazingly clear moving pictures of himself on a CCTV camera on the car park.

Savage's disappearance had been a thoroughly smooth job; no positive sightings of him had been made and there was a UK all-stations call-out for him. If he did turn up, he might be able to throw some light on the relationship between Doonan and Smith. As Angel was looking through the window, he also supposed he could see a herd of pigs flying past.

There was a knock at the door. It was Scrivens. He was clutching an armload of A4-size paper files to his chest.

'Is it convenient to see me, sir?'

'Come in, lad. I was wondering where you had got to.'

The files slid about precariously in Scrivens' arms as he closed the door.

'Put the stuff down there,' Angel said, pointing to the corner of his desk.

Scrivens was relieved to unload the files. 'Thank you, sir.' He placed them down carefully and squared them off.

Angel leaned towards him with eyes narrowed and said: 'Now, what have you got?'

Scrivens said, 'The computer geeks recovered all the work, including the deletions, Peter Santana had tapped into his three computers over the past month, sir, that is, since 15 November, and I have printed it all out. I have also printed out all of his files that were open on that date and since. And I must say, sir, that the bulk of it consists of scene after scene of scripts, with instructions for the characters and the cameraman. Also plots in abbreviated form. I suppose they were ideas and thoughts he had had as he was pressing along with writing other things. And then there were loads of short notes, obviously to remind him about something or to tell somebody to do something. And there are lists. And drafts of business letters. Boring stuff like insurance. And there's also—'

'Insurance? What's this with insurance, Ted?'

'He wanted to make changes. Increase the cover on the farmhouse up at Tunistone. I think it was insured for one and a half million, but he wanted to double it … increase it to three.'

Lot of money for a farmhouse, Angel thought, out in the wilds. Mind you, it had a swimming pool, lots of land, a magnificent view. But he wouldn't like to live there. Most of the year it would be too cold. He shuddered as he thought about it.

'It's in there, sir,' Scrivens said. 'As near as I can remember. Apparently there had been some earth movement, and the letter to his insurance broker said something about the risk of fire had therefore greatly increased. If electric cables were severed by earth movement, it could lead to explosion or fire … that sort of thing.'

Angel screwed his face up and rubbed his chin. 'I've not heard of any earth movement up there.'

'Nor have I, sir.'

Angel wrinkled his nose and sniffed. 'Anything else?'

'Yes, sir. I found the partial drafting of a will.'

Angel looked up. 'Really? What's that?'

'His will, sir. It looks like he intended changing it.'

'Right, lad. What were the changes? Who was to inherit what?'

Scrivens shuffled through a file, sorted out a sheet of A4 and handed it to him.

'It's not that straightforward,' Scrivens said. 'All his estate, at the time, was left to his wife, Felicity. He wanted to split it fifty-fifty and create "The Peter Santana Trust". He wrote: "I want the Trust to be run by a small committee, say three, with Bill Isaacs in the chair. It is to be for the benefit of writers/producers of original ideas who have the talent, but not the funds, to develop them and take them through to completed satisfying entertainment on tape or film."'

Angel took the sheet of paper and read the paragraph for himself.

'Is it significant, sir?'

'When did he write this?'

Scrivens looked at the cover of the file. 'Monday 8 December, sir.'

'Hmmm. It's significant that he was thinking about his last will and testament only a week before he was murdered. And that he must think well of Mr Isaacs.'

'He's the boss of the studio.'

'Was there anything about a pig?' asked Angel.

'Not much, really, sir.'

His face brightened. *Anything* was better than nothing. 'What is there?'

Out of the same file, Scrivens pulled out another sheet of A4 and handed it to him. 'It's just a simple list, sir. It was tapped out on the same day.'

It read:

ether
cotton wool
dead pig fresh 100 lbs
silk nightdress
Monday night next

Angel read it twice, then copied it out. When he had finished, he rubbed his chin and frowned.

'What's it mean, sir?' Scrivens said.

'Don't know, lad,' he said. 'Ether is a bit old-fashioned. Doctors and dentists used to use it as an anaesthetic. I am not aware of anything else you might use it for. The pig was dead so I can't see that he would want to anaesthetize it. A "dead pig, fresh, 100 lbs", is self-explanatory, as is a "silk nightdress".'

'Why do you think he decided on silk, sir?'

'Why indeed, lad? Why not cotton? It's cheaper. Does the same job on a dead pig. Covers it up. Silk might be more glamorous, but whatever you dressed a dead pig in wouldn't make it any the more interesting, would it?'

'And "Monday night next", what's the significance of that, sir?'

'I don't know what Santana intended it to mean. But ominously, that's the date when he was murdered,' he said.

'The pig, the nightdress and Monday night next were all to do with the crime scene at Tunistone, sir. But we didn't find any ether there' said Scrivens.

Angel stood up. 'I don't know,' he said and ran his hand through his hair. He walked up and down the little office with his hands behind his back. After a few moments he pointed to the pile of files and said, 'Are you certain there's nothing else in there about a pig?'

'Yes, sir.'

'Have you read it all?'

Scrivens hesitated. 'I've *looked* at everything, sir. I haven't always tried to understand it all.'

'Are you sure there's no plot or story involving a pig or a monkey or a tarantula, or anything else being dressed in a nightdress and put in a bed?'

'There's nothing like that in there, sir.'

'Right, lad,' he said. 'Leave it with me. I'll take it home. It'll be a little light reading for me over the weekend,' he added, blowing out a foot of air.

'I want you to understand that I have come here of my own free will,' Laurence Smith said in a powerful voice with an accent straight from the valleys.

But it wasn't true. The two uniformed men from DI Asquith's team had said that he was very argumentative and vocal, and that they had to use a lot of persuasion to get him out of his house into their car, and then when they arrived at the station more argument to get him out of their car and into the interview room.

'I hear what you say,' Angel said evenly.

'And furthermore,' Smith continued, 'I have no idea who this man sat next to me is. You tell me he is a solicitor acting for me, but he could be one of your coppers for all I know.'

Angel looked across the table at Mr Bloomfield and invited him to show Smith his credentials and hoped that in so doing some rapport may develop between the two of them, thus allowing them to move on to the interview.

Angel rose and left the table and Scrivens followed.

Bloomfield was a very experienced criminal solicitor. If he couldn't get Smith's confidence, nobody could.

The delay lasted only three minutes. Angel and Scrivens returned and were seated at the table opposite Smith and Bloomfield.

Angel switched on the recording machine and made the usual statement about persons present, the date and the time. After that, the first one to speak was Smith.

'I want it understood that I have no idea what I have been brought in here about, and that I have done nothing wrong.'

Bloomfield whispered something in his ear but Smith didn't reply or react.

Angel said: 'This is purely a preliminary inquiry, Mr Smith. The position simply is this: a man was murdered in the Fisherman's Rest pub on Canal Road last Tuesday, the sixteenth. You were picked out by a witness from over a hundred photographs that showed only part of the face. Mostly the eyes.'

'I wasn't there,' Smith said. 'It wasn't me.'

'The witness was only eighteen inches from the man's face,' Angel said.

'It wasn't me.'

'It's hardly likely he was mistaken.'

'It wasn't me. He may need glasses. I expect he was drunk.'

'He was stone cold sober. Where were you at nine o'clock?'

'I was at home.'

'Who with?'

'I was by myself. I live alone. Who would I be with? Huh.'

'Is there anybody who can support your story?'

'It's not a story. It's a fact, man. I was at home, alone. I live alone these days.'

Angel rubbed his chin. 'What were you doing?'

'I don't know now. Probably watching the box. There's nothing on, but I still look at the bloody thing. It's like a drug. Cheaper than Horlicks. Sends me to sleep.'

'You knew about the shooting?'

'I did. I read it in the paper. It's all fantasy. I also read all about you investigating the murder of that millionaire chap and the pig in the pink nightie. Huh. True life is better than TV any time, boyo.'

The muscles of Angel's jaw tightened. 'It's no fantasy,' he growled. 'And it's not a matter to joke about.'

'I was not joking. I am not laughing, am I?'

Angel stared at him. It was true. His face was as glum as ever. Smith never smiled.

'You knew the dead man,' Angel said. 'A friend of yours. His name was Vincent Doonan.'

'Yes. I knew him. A nasty, dishonest individual. No friend of mine.'

Angel's eyes flashed. 'He went down for the identical offence you did.'

'We may have relieved a public body of a small amount of its worn-out scrap wire—'

'You stole 120 yards of copper wire and brought chaos and misery for around thirty hours to thousands of passengers travelling on the main line from Kings Cross to Edinburgh.'

'But Vincent Doonan stole from me and from Harry Savage. We were partners. It was a monstrous, wicked thing to do to your mates.'

Angel's fists tightened. He must stay cool. 'What do you mean?'

'Doonan wasn't any good at arithmetic, you see. Apparently he had never learned how to divide by *three*. He knew how to divide by *four*, though, because he gave Harry Savage and me a fourth each, and himself two fourths, which I didn't think was quite right.'

Angel blinked when he heard him mention Harry Savage. He knew he needed to be found and arrested.

'Where is Harry these days?' Angel said lightly. 'Haven't seen him around.'

'Don't know about that, Inspector Angel. I give him a wide berth. Don't think I seen him twice since I come out of prison. Probably gone abroad for a rest.'

'Hmmm.' Angel rubbed his chin. 'Are you *sure* you didn't go to the Fisherman's Rest on Tuesday night?'

'Positive. I have no money for drinking, man.'

'What do you do with your money, then?'

'I don't have any. You know that. If I had any money it would go straight to Marie and the kids. A court order, Inspector Angel. You know all about court orders, don't you? If I earn any money, it goes straight to my wife and kids. I get nothing of it. I could never earn enough to pay off what I owe, so I am permanently in debt. I would have to be the Minister for Welsh Affairs or get moulded to look like Jordan to be able to afford to work again. My giro gives me just enough to keep me alive. The government knows this. They make the calculation. It's precariously close to the breadline, though.'

'You've money to spare to buy yourself a paper.'

'I read them free in the public library.'

'And you can afford a good suit.'

'It's a cut-down of my late father's funeral suit. Tailored perfectly by my dear mother.'

Angel rubbed his chin. 'Well, I am not satisfied with your explanation. I am going to hold you here until I have obtained a warrant and searched your house.'

Smith jumped to his feet. 'This is bloody outrageous!' he yelled.

Bloomfield reached up and tugged at his sleeve. 'Sit down. Please sit down.'

Smith ignored him. He stared at Angel and said: 'But I didn't do it. I wasn't there. Why don't you believe me?'

Angel stiffened. 'Because you said exactly the same thing when you were pulled in for stealing the copper wire. You said you didn't do it. Even when it was traced back to you and Doonan and Savage, even when we found your fingerprints on two places on the cable, even in court after you had taken the oath, you told lie after lie and kept on lying. It was only when the jury had found you guilty and I spoke to you in the court cells that you slyly, grudgingly admitted it. And that was because you thought I could influence the custodial board to send you to HMP Doncaster to be near your home instead of somewhere far away. Some hopes. That's why.'

Smith shrugged and shook his head. He knew it was true. Then he suddenly said, 'That doesn't make me a frigging murderer!'

Angel's lips tightened back against his teeth. He looked across at him and said, 'If you didn't do it, you've nothing to worry about, have you?' Then he leaned over to the recording control panel. 'Interview ended 1621 hours,' he said, then he switched off the tape, turned to Scrivens and said, 'Search him, get the keys to his house and take him down to a cell.'

CHAPTER 7

It was forty minutes later. The time was five o'clock and Angel was on the phone.

'It's just a superficial search, Don. It's only a two-up and two-down. There'll be three of us. Shouldn't take more than half an hour. Ed Scrivens has the key, and I've a man getting the warrant at this very minute. He should be back here in five minutes literally.'

'Right, sir,' Taylor said. 'Better phone my wife.' He replaced the phone.

Angel reflected a moment and decided that he would do the same. He tapped in the number.

'Hello, love, it's me. I'll be an hour or so late. Something's cropped up.'

'It's nothing dangerous, Michael, is it?' asked Mary.

'No. No. Nothing like that. Nothing to worry about.'

'All right. I can hold tea back until 6.30. Have you thought any more about Timmy?'

He ran his hand through his hair. 'Timmy? What's Timmy?'

'*Timmy!*' she bawled. 'My godson, Timothy, of course.'

He felt the heat of Mary's impatience burn its way down the telephone wire.

'Oh, him. Getting married. What is there to think about?'

'A present. We'll *have* to buy them a present.'

'Oh yes. Send them money.'

'You know we can't do that. Can't send *money* for a wedding present. It's so … so vulgar.'

Vulgar. He wished his friends, relations and enemies had been so vulgar when they were married. 'What sort of thing do you mean?'

'Something nice.'

'Yes,' he said. He hadn't an idea in his head. They probably expected a bungalow. 'I can't think of anything, Mary,' he said. 'I have to go.'

'Well, think about it,' she said. 'Be careful. Goodbye.'

It was 6 p.m. when a constable arrived back at the station from Doctor Jenkins, a Justice of the Peace, with a signed warrant. Thereafter, the three policemen, Angel, Taylor and Scrivens, promptly made their way in the BMW through the cold, black night to 36 Sebastopol Terrace, a dingy little terraced house, the home of Laurence Smith.

Sebastopol Terrace was one of four long parallel rows of tiny houses squashed together back to back. The estate had been built by the owner of the local coalmine in the 1890s to a basic specification to provide cheap housing for their workmen and families. More than a hundred years later, while the shell of the buildings remained substantial, other parts of the houses, from the damp courses to the chimney pots, were generally in need of attention.

The Sebastopol estate had become a cowboy property repairer's paradise.

Angel turned the key in the door of the unlit gloomy house and the three policemen bustled in out of the cold with their torches showing them the way. Taylor made straightaway for the staircase to the upper floor. Scrivens went straight ahead where he assumed the kitchen would be.

As Angel found the light switch, he immediately became aware of the lavish furnishings and décor. The little front room was crammed with modern, comfortable furniture, a huge, slimline TV set, ingenious imitation coal-effect fire in the hearth and a well-stocked mini-bar. He didn't delay. He began by turning over the easy chair, looking for any interference with any part of the upholstery. It seemed to be untouched. He was turning it back when Scrivens wandered back into the room with his mouth open.

Angel looked up and their eyes met. He reckoned that they were thinking the same thing. What they had discovered was a lot different from the impression Laurence Smith had tried to convey: that he was the poverty-stricken ex-husband suffering from a grasping wife, the injustices of the divorce law and the deficiencies of the welfare state.

Scrivens nodded knowingly. 'You should see the kitchen, sir. Must have cost thousands.'

Angel stopped what he was doing and followed Scrivens through.

The kitchen was newly tiled and fitted out with all new domestic machinery, equipment and furniture, and a streamlined central heating boiler was on the wall feeding a system that was keeping the house pleasantly warm that cold December night.

'Where did he get his money from then, sir?'

Angel shook his head. 'I don't know, lad. I don't know.'

Taylor searched the bedroom and bathroom carefully. He had been briefed specifically to look for a black or navy blue woollen hat and scarf. He searched the chest of drawers, the wardrobe, pillows and mattress. He removed the boxed area that surrounded the bath; he tapped every upstairs floor-board to see if any were loose; he checked the fitted carpet to see if it was not neatly fixed in any place. He looked behind everything hanging on the walls. Meanwhile Scrivens found the tiny pantry and looked in every unsealed jar and every opened packet, and checked the seals of everything unopened to confirm the contents.

All three policemen looked in every conceivable nook and cranny and failed to find any incriminating evidence that showed the involvement of Laurence Smith in the murder of Vincent Doonan, or indeed an involvement in any other crime.

An hour later they met up in the kitchen. Their sober expressions and minimal crosstalk exemplified their disappointment at finding nothing in their searches.

Suddenly there was the whirring sound from the mechanism of a cuckoo clock on the wall behind them beginning its hourly cycle.

Angel recognized the noise and he turned round to look at the unusual timepiece, his eyes wide open.

Scrivens and Taylor watched the clock with amused eyes until the cuckoo retired through its tiny doors for the last time, having declared that the time was seven o'clock.

Angel shook his head. He was quietly surprised that every house in Bromersley seemed to have one.

'A great novelty,' Taylor said. 'But you must eventually get fed up with the noise?'

Angel nodded and with another key from Smith's bunch, he unlocked the back door leading out to the tiny backyard. It had originally been a place to set up a clothesline. At the farthest extent, next to a tumbledown gate in the boundary wall, was a brick building adjoining a similar building in next door's yard, which was divided into two and had a lavatory in each. Next to that was a coal bunker, and next to that and nearest the back door was a small hut locked with a padlock.

Scrivens went straight down to search the lavatory, Taylor peered into the coal bunker with a torch and Angel found another key and was soon unhooking the padlock from the hasp. In the hut he found a bag of builders' tools including a set of brush and rods such as those used to release blocked drains. There was also a pair of trainers and, hanging on a cup hook, some dirty overalls, and at the back of the hut was a large plastic bag.

Angel pulled it out, opened it up and looked inside. There were twenty or thirty tennis balls inside. He nodded knowingly and gave the bag to Scrivens. 'Take that, lad. Look after it. It's evidence.'

Scrivens blinked in the torchlight. 'Tennis balls? Evidence, sir?'

Scrivens unlocked the cell door and then stood back.

Angel walked inside. 'Right, you are free to go,' he said. 'If you go to the desk sergeant, you can collect the contents of your pockets.'

Laurence Smith glared at Angel as he eased himself off the bunkbed. 'I should never have been brought here in the first place.'

Angel's fists tightened. 'I am not yet satisfied that you had nothing to do with the death of Vincent Doonan, and there might be charges brought against you in connection with other unrelated offences. This release is conditional. You must not leave Bromersley without advising this office, and you must not visit the Fisherman's Rest. Understood?'

Smith frowned but didn't reply.

Angel said, '*Understood*?'

'Yeah. Yeah. All right. Understood.'

He stepped out of the cell. 'What did you say the name of that witness was … that was supposed to have picked me out?'

Nobody caught Angel out as easily as that.

'I didn't say,' he said as he closed the cell door and indicated the way out of the security block.

As they made their way up the corridor, Smith suddenly said: 'What unrelated offences?'

'The tennis ball scam, for one thing.'

'Don't know what you mean.'

Angel sighed.

They reached the duty sergeant's desk. There was nobody there. He must have been called away.

'Oh yes, you do,' Angel said. 'Your hut had a bag full of tennis balls in there. I have taken them and recorded them as evidence for the future. Don't even *think* of buying any more.'

'Oh yes,' Smith said. 'But they're not mine. They are for my nephews. They play with them when they visit me.'

Angel's eyes flashed. He was tired. It had been a long day. 'Don't tell me any more lies,' he said. 'You haven't got any nephews *or* nieces … or brothers or sisters, for that matter. I know that from your notes. So don't take me for a fool.'

He ran his hand through his hair and turned to Scrivens. 'It's late, Ted. I'm going home. Finish up here. See that Mr Smith is offered some transport. He might want some milk and a rusk. And he likes fairytales. If you have to, tell him the one about the three bears.'

'Go to *frigging hell!*' Smith yelled.

'Good night, sir,' Scrivens said.

The front door slammed. Angel had gone.

The phone rang.

Angel reached out for it. It was WPC Leisha Baverstock at reception. 'Good morning, sir. There's a young woman here asking to see you. Says her name is Sonya Quigley.'

Angel looked up. He didn't expect that. Sonya Quigley? Of course he would see her. 'Bring her down to my office, Leisha, please?'

He replaced the phone slowly and rubbed his chin. He wondered what she wanted. She might be able to throw some light on the murder of Doonan even though her father, Liam Quigley, was now out of the frame. Any relevant information would be most welcome. The investigation was going nowhere, and at that moment there was no way that he was able to prove the murderer was Laurence Smith.

Angel had always made it a rule that if anybody came to the station and asked for him by name, he would see them. Same thing if they phoned and asked for him – he would always speak to them.

Anyway, this young woman might be in trouble.

She arrived. She looked nothing like her father. She was pretty and slim, with long, red, stringy hair, and she wore a red coat over jeans and a thick white jumper. She glanced at Angel but didn't maintain a long look.

'Good morning. You are Sonya Quigley? Please sit down.'

'Yes. Thank you,' she said.

She had skinny, children's fingers, which she played with as she spoke.

'Daughter of Liam Quigley? What can I do for you?' Angel said.

'Yes. I'd like to see him, please.'

Angel frowned. 'He's not here, Sonya. Isn't he at home?'

Her eyes narrowed. 'Oh? He's not here? I thought he had been arrested?'

'He's probably at home now. Have you not been home?'

She put her elbows on the desk and buried her face in her hands. 'The next-door neighbour said that the police had taken him away and that he had been arrested. He wasn't there night before last.'

'He was released yesterday morning. He was only held here overnight for questioning.'

She sighed deeply. 'Oh, thank God. Thank God.' She found a tissue and began to wipe her cheeks. 'I thought he had been arrested for Vincent's murder. I knew he hadn't done it. He was angry, worked up if ever I mentioned his name, but I knew he couldn't take a man's life like that.'

Angel licked his bottom lip thoughtfully. 'What do you know about it, Sonya?'

The tears started again. 'Oh, it's all my fault, Mr Angel. Vincent never meant anything more to me than a safe place I could run to. I only went there to get away from Dad's moods, drunkenness and bad temper. He thinks I went to bed with him, but I never. Vincent was a nice enough chap, but not in that way … and he's old enough to be my father. I let my father think anything he wanted. I did it to annoy him … get my own back, you know. Vincent let me have his back bedroom whenever I wanted it, that's all, honest. He enjoyed my company … and I enjoyed his, when I was lonely or … afraid. But I never intended it to go this far with my Dad. Now I want to find him and tell him everything. I'm so relieved. Don't you know where he'll be now?'

Angel shook his head gently. 'I'm sorry.'

She suddenly pulled a face. 'He's started up with this Juanita Freedman woman. That's where he'll be. It's all so … awful!'

The tears started again.

Angel said, 'I've met Miss Freedman. She seemed pleasant enough.'

'He had me take her out … and entertain her. Just the two of us. Last night. To The Feathers. He shoved forty quid in my hand and said give her a good time and enjoy yourselves, and don't come back before eleven o'clock. She likes white wine. Oooh. Horrible stuff. I did it because he wanted me to. But I don't like it. All she talks about is books, Clarice Cliff, Rennie Mackintosh and Scotland … and she smells of peppermint. We got a taxi there and a taxi back. She's trying to take my mother's place. It's not right. Nobody can do that.'

'Of course not. Where's your mother?'

'She's in County Clare. Middle of nowhere. I love her dearly. I sometimes wish I was there with her and my grandmother. And my older sister.'

'You can always go back there, can't you?'

'I've been back. But there are no people there. Just women, and hens and sheep. It's like a graveyard and besides, there's no work. I couldn't easily settle after all this busy, busy over here. No. Besides, my father is trying to buy another house. It includes a shop. If he gets it … maybe … I can have the shop and start up as a hairdresser. I'm trained for that, you know. Been to Bromersley College. Got the diploma. Worked for a year at Madam Georgina's in town, you know.

But it'll never happen. You see. That woman'll be in the way. She'll put the mockers on it. You see.'

'Your mother?'

'No. Miss Juanita bloody Freedman.'

Ahmed came in and closed the door. 'You want me, sir?'

'Yes, lad. I want you to get that small ad in the Personal Column of the *South Yorkshire Post* all editions tomorrow night,' Angel said, passing him a small piece of paper.

Ahmed peered at the paper, frowned and looked across the desk at Angel.

Angel's mouth tightened. 'What's the matter? Can't you read it?'

'Yes, sir,' he said, then he cleared his throat and slowly read: 'Cherub wants love. Contact in usual way.'

'Yes, that's right,' Angel said loudly. 'Don't read it as if it's Japanese. It's perfectly good English.'

'Right, sir.'

'And tell them to charge it to me.'

'Yes, sir.'

Ahmed went out, re-reading the paper and shaking his head.

Angel watched the door close. He gave way to a smile as he considered what was going through Ahmed's mind.

He returned to the morning's post.

There was a knock at the door.

'Come in,' Angel called.

It was Gawber.

Angel looked up from his desk. 'Oh, it's you,' he said with eyebrows raised. 'Come in, Ron. I thought you'd run off and joined a circus.'

Gawber looked down at him and smiled. 'I've not been as long as all that, sir,' he said as he closed the office door. 'And I have caught up with some of the people in the Fisherman's Rest who *didn't* stay behind to be interviewed.'

Angel nodded appreciatively. He was really very pleased to see his favourite sergeant. He hoped that Gawber might cheer him up.

'I'm impressed, Ron,' he said. He moved the report he was reading on to a pile on the corner of the desk, leaned back and folded his arms. 'Well, I hope you know something helpful. I'm making absolutely zero progress here. And being rapidly worn down by the persistent ridicule from the newspapers about pigs in pokes, and every ham joke and pun about pigs, millionaires and glamorous widows you can possibly think of.'

'Huh. I've read them, sir,' Gawber said. 'You've never let the papers bother you before.'

'Well, ordinarily they wouldn't, if I knew we were making some progress, but we're not. Anyway, what have you got?'

Gawber pulled out his notebook and sighed. 'Nothing much. I first interviewed the three men who were sitting around the table with Doonan – separately, of course. They agreed on what he wore, the woolly hat, scarf and black gloves … and about what happened. Man came in, looked round, went to the bar, ordered a drink and a sandwich and when Clem Bailey went in the back to make the sandwich, he came over to them, pulled the gun out of his pocket, pointed it at Vincent Doonan, pulled the trigger three times then went straight out through the door. It was as quick and simple as that.'

'It seems to me that the murderer knew that Clem Bailey would have to go in the room behind the bar to make up the sandwich. He wanted him out of the way. Why?'

'Because he thought Bailey might recognize him, or because he thought he might have tried to prevent him.'

'Not much you can do against a determined man with a loaded gun. It must have been because he thought he might recognize him.'

Gawber nodded. 'Perhaps he didn't want to be in Clem Bailey's sights for too long?'

Angel nodded, then he said, 'You know that Clem Bailey picked out Laurence Smith from the mug book?'

Gawber's mouth opened and his eyebrows went up.

'But we can't make it stick,' Angel added quickly.

'He's got a good alibi?'

'No. He hasn't got *any* alibi. He hasn't got a strong enough motive either. Some argument over a shareout of the spoils of an old job. CPS would never take it on. Go on. Tell me. What else?'

'Remember there was a family of five, the Summervilles, three women and two men, who were in the pub at the time of the murder? Well, one of the men, father Summerville, came into the pub yesterday lunchtime ... started talking to Clem about the murder. By chance, I called in on Clem Bailey and Clem pointed him out to me. I had a word with him, took his address and his sister's address and was able to interview all of them. Apparently it had been his wife's birthday. The family were out for a celebratory drink.'

'What did they see?'

'Mr Summerville senior said that he was side on to the gun and he reckons he knows about arms. It was his hobby until the laws about owning guns and the banning of replicas was introduced in the eighties. He said that he saw the silhouette of the barrel. Unusual design. The finger guard almost reached the end of the barrel. Also, the gun had a blue tinge and therefore he believes it was a Beretta Tomcat.'

Angel blinked. That was interesting. 'It's true, but it could also have been stainless steel or titanium. Do you think he's reliable?'

'He seemed to be talking sense to me, sir.'

Angel rubbed his chin and said, 'The calibre of a Beretta is .32.' He reached out for the phone and determinedly tapped in the number to the mortuary at Bromersley General.

Gawber said, 'Have you heard back from Dr Mac about the—'

'I'm going to find that out, right now,' he said.

The phone was answered. 'Mac? It's Michael Angel. Sorry to bother you, but I haven't had your report on either Doonan or Santana yet, and I—'

Dr Mac said, 'I know. I know. I've done the work, it's just a matter of—'

'All I want to know just now is the calibre of the three bullets that went into Vincent Doonan.'

'I can remember that. They were from the same gun, of course, and they were .32.'

'.32, Mac? Thank you very much.'

Angel and Gawber exchanged looks.

He replaced the phone. 'So we know the murder weapon. Now we know what we're looking for.'

'Yes, but it might be at the bottom of the Don, sir.'

'It might. It might not.'

The phone rang. Angel reached out for it. It was the super.

'Yes, sir?' Angel said and wrinkled his nose.

'You'd better come up here,' Harker growled. 'Straightaway,' he added and there was a loud click.

Angel groaned and slammed down the receiver. He turned to Gawber and said, 'I've got to go.'

Gawber stood up. 'I've to write up my notes. I'll carry on, if you don't need me.'

'Right,' Angel said, feeling briefly quite envious of him.

They both went out of the office. Gawber dashed out next door into the CID office, while Angel charged up the green corridor.

He didn't know what Harker wanted. It must be something in a report he wanted to ask about. He was surely not going to bellyache about the fact that he hadn't yet charged anybody for either of the murders. It wasn't a week since Santana had been found murdered and only three days since Doonan had been shot dead.

He arrived at Harker's door, tapped on it and walked in. It reeked of menthol and it was uncomfortably hot. It was like being in a greenhouse in July with all the windows shut.

The pasty-faced ogre with the big eyebrows and the cough was seated at a desk, peering at him between two piles of files and papers.

'You're there, Angel,' he muttered. 'Sit down.' He snatched an A5 sheet of pink paper from out of a wire basket and peered at it.

Angel thought he recognized it. From where he was sitting, it looked like an expense chitty.

Harker glared at the paper and said, 'You seem to have an obsession with cuckoo clocks. So much so that you couldn't resist the infantile urge to go out and buy one.'

Angel sniffed. It *was* an expense chitty. It was *his* expense chitty.

'It wasn't like that at all, sir.'

'With police funds.'

'I bought it, sir, because it seemed odd that all round the town just about every villain I have called on in the past week has one on his wall.'

'So you thought, hang the expense. It's not my money. You didn't want to be left out.'

'No, sir. In view of your observations about large quantities of heroin arriving in all kinds of unusual containers, I thought it possible that maybe the stuff was being smuggled inside the clocks.'

'Yes. I know. As well as shelling out police funds, you committed police facilities – costly, valuable police facilities – to examine the damned thing.'

His eyebrows went up. 'I did ask SOCO to—'

'Well, I have instructed DS Taylor to return the thing to you forthwith as it was. Really, Angel, I sometimes think you've gone round the twist. SOCO can't examine every damned pot, pan or clock that tickles your fancy on the off-chance that it may contain drugs, and so that you can have a free handout in the process. They have far too much to do.'

'I've never put forward an item to be examined for drugs before, sir. You are suggesting that I am always calling on the facilities of SOCO to examine things. It is not for my personal benefit. It was simply to try to curb the illegal import of drugs, heroin in particular. That's all.'

'I think, lad, that you're getting away from the main thrust of your responsibility at this station.'

Angel felt his face getting hot. 'Detecting crime and bringing criminals to justice is what I thought I was supposed to be doing.'

'Detecting crimes of *murder* is what *you're* supposed to be doing, lad. Specifically, solving and bringing to court the two cases I have given you. Murder is what you're supposed to be good at. The newspapers are always singing your praises. I daresay if they knew the truth, about your stupid diversions into cuckoo clocks and other crackpot things, they wouldn't glorify you so much.'

The muscles on Angel's jaw tightened. A regular banging started in his chest and extended to a throbbing in his ears. He wanted to let rip but it would only have lost him his job … the job he loved more than anything in the world. He tried to marshal his thoughts. He couldn't think of anything to say that was reverential and useful. His mind could only produce words of anger.

'Let's move on,' Harker said. 'This Santana case … It is giving the newspapers a field day. I am fed up with jibes and cartoons of pigs in nightdresses and uniformed policemen standing by scratching their heads. This really is too bad. It brings disgrace on the force. When are you prepared to issue a statement to shut them up?'

Angel clenched his fists. There was truth in what Harker had said. He couldn't deny it.

I know, sir. I can only issue a statement when I have something new to say. These newspaper men are not fools. If I tried to waffle on telling them general stuff that they already know, it would only annoy them and stir it all up even more. They want answers … to the key questions.'

'As a matter of fact, lad, I wouldn't mind knowing the answers to those questions myself. When are you going to be able to come up with some answers?'

Angel had no glib reply, no clever comeback. All he could say was, 'I don't know, sir. I don't know.'

Five minutes later, he came out of the super's office, his heart pounding like a timpanist playing Tchaikovsky. He stormed down the corridor to his office, bounded in and closed the door much louder than he had intended.

CHAPTER 8

It was a few minutes before he could resume any kind of work that required creative or original thought and, providentially, it was at the end of that interval of time that there was a knock at his office door.

He licked his lips, breathed in and then out and called, 'Come in.'

It was DS Taylor, head of SOCO. He was carrying a cardboard box under his arm. He closed the door.

When Angel saw who it was, his jaw dropped open. He stared up at him. 'It's you,' he said through contorted lips. 'What have you been telling the super?'

Taylor looked back awkwardly and said, 'Before you say anything, sir, I must tell you that it was not my fault.'

Angel continued to stare at him.

Taylor, still holding the cardboard box, said, 'About twenty minutes ago, the super asked me if my team had completed all the investigations that you had asked for in connection with both murder cases and I said that we had, which was true. He then asked me what we were busy with at that time. So I said that we were examining a cuckoo clock that you had brought in. I couldn't say anything different, sir. That was the truth. Well, he went straight up in the air.

I had no chance to explain anything to him. He went ballistic. When he came down, he said that I was to call my boys off, put the clock back in its wrapping and return it to you forthwith.'

Angel's breathing slowed.

He appreciated the fact that Taylor couldn't have avoided obeying the superintendent and he gestured with a single finger to put the box down on his desk.

'So in that box is a cuckoo clock,' Angel said, 'which you are duly returning to me, in pieces, which may or may not have hidden compartments to aid the smuggling of heroin or some other illegal substance?'

'Not quite, sir.'

'Oh?'

'Several things, sir. The clock is fully assembled and in perfect working order and keeps time pretty well. We had already checked it out. And I can confirm that there are no concealed compartments and no chemical traces of any kind of known illegal drugs or substances.'

'The bird thing that pops out?'

'Wood and plastic on a spring. Nothing unusual.'

'And the weights. What are they made of?'

'Pig iron, sir. We have drilled a tiny hole right through. We have tested the dust. It is the crudest, cheapest, heaviest pig iron you can find. We have then filled the holes up to match the original weight and covered the very slight damage with a dab of brown paint.'

'What about the packaging?'

'It's a simple cardboard box, sir, not excessive. Nothing unusual. Just the right amount of packing, I would say, for an item of that weight, size and kind being transported across Europe that distance by air.'

Angel pursed his lips. 'You're certain about that?'

'Stake my reputation on it.'

It seemed that Angel's idea that the cuckoo clocks were being used to smuggle heroin or other illegal substances was unfounded: he could surely rely on Don Taylor not to let anything get past him in that regard. Nevertheless, there was some reason why the town was flooded with them at such a ridiculously low price.

'Right,' Angel said. 'Thank you. You've done your best. Hop off. We'll leave it at that.'

Taylor sighed. He was very relieved. He went out much happier than he had come in.

Angel opened the flaps of the cardboard box and looked in at the clock carefully wrapped in polythene, with the weights slotted into folded cardboard sections inserted one each at two of the four corners for protection of the mechanism. He closed the flaps, and read the label. Then he reached out for the phone to summon Gawber.

A few minutes later, Gawber came into the office.

'You wanted me, sir?' he said.

Angel pointed at the box on his desk. 'That's one of those clocks, Ron,' he said. 'Don Taylor says that clock case is hiding *nothing* ... no heroin ... no illegal substance ... not so much as a hint of a wine gum ... but I'm still not satisfied.' He began to read from the label on the flap. 'From the Tikka Tokka Cuckoo Clock Company, Mingenstrasse, Reebur, Switzerland. To the Antique Shop, Bull's Foot Railway Arches, Wath Road, Bromersley, South Yorkshire, UK. 1 of a consignment of 250.' He looked up at him. 'I want you to get on to this, Ron. Find out what you can about this factory in Switzerland. Pretend you own a chain of novelty shops or something and you want to buy a couple of million clocks. Then give them a ring. That should make them concentrate their attention on you, break off sliding down mountains on their Toblerones, yodelling and singing about Maria and the lonely goat herd.'

Angel was in his office, reading the transcript of the statement made by Laurence Smith.

The phone rang. He reached out for it. It was Crisp.

Angel's eyebrows shot up. 'About time I heard from you. Where are you, lad? Have you emigrated?'

Crisp's jaw dropped. '*No, sir.* I'm in the film studio. Got a job as a sound engineer.'

Angel frowned. 'Oh? What exactly is that?'

'I hold a pole and follow people round.'

Angel frowned. 'I hope you're spending the government's money wisely, lad?'

'Can't stay, sir. I've made contact with Felicity Santana's gofer, Marianne Cooper. She's a bit too young for me, sir, but she's got this ravishing hair, and legs that …'

Angel sighed. 'I'm not interested in what she looks like,' he yelled.

Crisp's tone changed. 'No, sir. Sorry, sir. I wanted to tell you about this handgun, sir. It was in the men's washroom. He dropped it on the floor. Two minutes ago. He picked it up and put it in his right jacket pocket. His name is Samson Fairchild.'

'Who is he?'

'He's an actor. Very well known, sir.'

Angel hadn't heard of him. 'Hmmm. Was that gun real or a replica?'

'Looked real to me, sir. Anyway there's no gun play in the film he's in.'

'Did he see you?'

'Don't think so.'

'Right, lad. I'll deal with it. Better get back to the girl with the ravishing … whatever it was.'

'I don't care who you are, sir,' the gate man at the Top Hat Film Studios said. 'You're not allowed past this barrier without a pass. It's regulations. Health and safety, you know.'

Angel leaned out of the car window. 'Come here, little man.'

The burly six foot uniformed gate man leaned down to Angel's car window.

Angel grabbed him by the tie and pulled him up to three inches from his nose and said, 'I've shown you my warrant card with my ID and photograph in it, my police badge, and I've told you I'm on very urgent business. If you value *your* health and safety, you'll lift that barrier double quick or you'll be arrested for obstructing the police in the execution of their duty.'

The gate man swallowed. His face stretched the length of a truncheon. 'Oh yes, sir. Right, sir,' he said. 'I didn't realize …'

Angel released the grip of his tie.

The barrier shot up.

'Where will I find Samson Fairchild?' he said.

'Second sound stage. Second on your left, sir. Got a big "2" painted on it. Don't say I told you.'

Angel let in the clutch and the BMW sped straight ahead into the concrete wonderland. It was an area the size of three football pitches comprising huge, single-storey buildings criss-crossed with wide concrete service lanes. There were signs everywhere, more than the inside of a prison. They were on buildings and on signposts in the middle of the concrete lanes. '5 mph.' 'No Smoking.' 'No Waiting.' 'No Stopping.' 'No Parking.' 'No horns to be used.' 'No left turn.' 'No right turn.' 'Sound Stage 1.' 'Sound Stage 2.' 'Canteen.' 'Props.' 'Admin.' 'Make-Up.' 'Car Park.'

There was nobody about, and no vehicles on the move. Angel passed two large buildings, Administration and Sound Stage 1, and reached a bigger building marked Sound Stage 2. He stopped the car by the door and rushed into the building. He had to pass through two lots of double doors before he was actually inside the studio itself, which was a huge single floor space with a high roof. There was a conglomeration of scenery in the middle with batteries of powerful lights, cameras and cables and about forty people standing around looking at a small area in front of a section of scenery. That was where the filming was taking place.

As Angel approached, he could hear a lone, male, theatrical voice offering his life and love to somebody in a very beautiful dress. He realized that he was the only person moving about, that everyone else was standing stock-still and so quiet you could have heard a £10 note drop into a screw's pocket.

More than twenty lights were directed on the actor, some at very close quarters. Everybody's attention was on the man, addressing a woman seated on a sofa who Angel recognized as Felicity Santana. Then the actor stopped speaking. There were a few seconds of silence then a voice through an amplification system called out, 'Cut. That's OK. Print it. Break for tea. Ten minutes, no longer.'

Powerful lights went out with a whoosh, loud chattering started, hammering began, technicians wheeled cameras and apparatus to another set and many feet made for the exit, some to the canteen, the executives to their offices and the star actors to their luxury caravans.

Angel saw Crisp rushing past. He was carrying a microphone on a pole. They exchanged glances but nothing more.

Nobody seemed to notice Angel's presence; they were each occupied with their own job. He approached the man who had issued the instructions through the loudspeaker system. He was writing something on a clipboard.

'Excuse me,' Angel said. 'I want to speak to Samson Fairchild.'

'Everybody does,' the young man said, then he looked up. He stared at Angel. 'Who are you?' he added with unfriendly eyes. 'I don't know you. Where's your pass? You shouldn't be in here.'

'I'm Detective Inspector Angel from Bromersley police. I am investigating the murder of Peter Santana.'

The man's eyebrows shot up. 'Oh? I didn't know about you being here. I'm very sorry,' he said. 'I am the floor manager, Oliver Razzle. Mr Fairchild will be in his caravan.' He tossed the clipboard on to a chair. 'I'm going in that direction. I'll take you across there.'

The building had emptied except for a gang of men setting up lighting banks, standards and other equipment in a different part of the studio. There were only Angel and

Razzle striding out across the set to a row of four American RVs parked up close to the wall.

'How is the investigation going, Inspector? Mr Santana was highly regarded here, you know. We hope that you will soon find his killer.'

'We will,' Angel said, trying to sound confident. 'It's only a matter of time.'

Angel always said that. In the past, it had always been true. He hoped that this time would be no exception.

They arrived outside one of the big caravans. The words 'Mr Samson Fairchild' were painted on the door. Razzle pointed to it.

'Thank you,' Angel said. 'I'll need to have a word with you later.'

Razzle looked at his watch. 'We'll be through shooting at four. Early finish Friday. If that would be convenient.'

'Fine,' Angel said.

'My office then. Anyone will direct you. Four o'clock.'

Angel nodded, but he was anxious to meet up with the man with the gun before anyone was hurt.

Razzle went out through the exit door.

Angel looked at the big American RV and knocked on the door. He didn't know what to expect. Crisp had simply told him that a man called Samson Fairchild had a gun in his coat pocket. Fairchild could be a raving lunatic, a man on the run … anything could happen. He licked his lips. The door handle rattled. The door opened outwards. Angel took a deep breath. A tall, broad-shouldered man with a gold suntan appeared; he stood at the top of the steps posing like a statue. His suit was as sleek as the bodywork of a Maserati.

Fairchild didn't lower his head. He looked down at him with eyelids almost closed. 'Yes?' he said in a bored, superior voice.

'Mr Fairchild? DI Angel, Bromersley police. I am looking into the murder of Peter Santana. Can I have a word, sir?'

'Oh?' Fairchild said, with eyebrows raised. 'I suppose so. Of course. Come on in.' He held the door open.

Angel leaped quickly up the three steps with rather too much momentum and stumbled against the right side of the man rather clumsily, pushing him back against a large cupboard just inside the doorway. For a moment he was pressed unpleasantly close against him.

'Steady on there,' Fairchild said. 'Mind the suit.'

'I am so very sorry, sir,' Angel said eventually, straightening up and pulling himself away.

Fairchild gave him a superior look. 'That's all right,' he said gruffly. He closed the caravan door, and turned back to face the policeman.

Angel raised a Walther PPK/S between finger and thumb in his left hand, pulled a pencil out of his top pocket, placed it down the barrel, held the gun aloft on the pencil and checked to see if it was loaded. It was. He could see the rim of a bullet in the breech. He held it to his nose and sniffed. The giveaway smell of burning indicated that it had been fired recently.

Fairchild stared at the gun. His eyes flashed. His jaw dropped. He dived frantically into his jacket pocket. It was empty. His eyes flashed again. 'What are you doing with that?'

Angel stared back at him. He held the Walther up again and said, 'Have you got a licence for this, sir?'

The pupils of Fairchild's eyes zipped to the left, to the right and back again, before finally settling somewhere in the centre. 'It's not mine.'

'It was in your possession. Don't you know it's a criminal offence to own a gun or even a replica, and this isn't a replica.'

He shook his head. 'I know you'll never believe it,' he said, 'but I found it.'

'Found it? Where?'

'In the men's washroom, an hour ago.'

Angel reached inside his pocket and pulled out a polythene 'EVIDENCE' bag he had brought for the occasion. He tilted the pencil and the gun slid gently off it into the bag; he sealed it and stuffed it into his pocket. He could hardly wait to get it into SOCO's hands.

Fairchild had watched him. He blinked several times and said, 'It will have my fingerprints on it.'

'That's all right,' Angel said. He looked round the caravan. His gaze settled on the sink next to a fridge and between them on the floor was a plastic rubbish bin. He crossed over to it. It seemed to be filled mostly with empty bottles; he fished around and found an empty gin bottle. He pulled it out triumphantly and turned to Fairchild, who had been closely watching him and who now stood there looking at him with a downturned mouth and raised eyebrows.

'Have you any gin, Mr Fairchild?'

The man stared hard at him. 'It is too early in the day for me, sir,' he said.

Angel shook his head. He knew what he was thinking. 'I need it to clean this bottle,' he said slowly and with emphasis. 'Then I'll have a perfect surface to take your fingerprints for elimination.'

Fairchild's mouth dropped open. After a moment, he pointed to a cupboard above the sink. 'There's almost a full bottle in there.'

'Do you mind if I take a half tumbler full and some tissues?'

Fairchild nodded his approval.

Angel quickly cleaned the empty bottle systematically with tissues sodden in gin, holding it with a finger in the top. Then he finished off the cleansing by wiping it carefully with a spotless tea towel hanging on a rail by the sink, carefully keeping his hand and fingers away from the glass surface. When he had finished, holding the bottle by a finger in the spout, he placed it on the draining board at the side of the sink and looked back at Fairchild.

'Now I want you to put your hands around the bottle, one above the other. I don't want you to slide about the glass – you'll smudge it. I want you simply to get a hold of the bottle with both hands at the same time, one each side, and grip it tight, then carefully peel your fingers off as you let go.'

Fairchild did it perfectly.

Angel smiled. 'May I put the bottle in this cupboard? I have other interviews to conduct. May I leave it here until I leave?'

'Certainly, Inspector. Collect it whenever you like. I will leave my caravan unlocked.'

Angel carefully reached up with his finger in the neck of the bottle and a fingertip underneath and placed it on the shelf along with several other bottles of booze. He closed the cupboard door and turned back to Fairchild. 'Now, you had better show me where you found the gun.'

Fairchild led him out of the caravan to the gentleman's washroom. He took him to the WC cubicle at the end of six. He said that he found the Walther on top of the cistern, partly concealed under a reserve toilet roll.

There was a sign behind the washroom door that gave an internal phone number to ring in case the toilets were not to a satisfactory standard. Angel prompted Fairchild to ring the number from a telephone outside in the corridor. A man with a cleaning trolley appeared promptly. Angel ascertained from him that the washroom and each cubicle had been checked and rinsed by him at two o'clock. He confirmed that the gun had not been there then. Angel thanked him, then he looked up and down the corridors close by for CCTV cameras, but there weren't any. He frowned.

Angel pushed open the door back into the studio, where the filming had re-started. Angel and Fairchild approached the caravan quietly.

When inside and seated, Angel said, 'Why didn't you report the finding of the gun?'

'I intended to, eventually, but I suppose to have it in my possession gave me a sense of security. It is pretty obvious that Peter Santana's murderer is someone in this studio, you know. It is somebody I work with every day. There's a sense of distrust arisen here, which I find very strange. And I ask myself, why was the gun left here, in the studio, when it could have been dumped almost anywhere?'

Angel gave a slight shrug. 'There are hundreds of questions, Mr Fairchild. I have to try to find the answers.'

He sensed that Fairchild had more to say. He leaned back in the comfortable chair in the caravan and waited.

'I should have thought as a detective,' Fairchild began, 'you would have been perfectly aware that since Peter Santana was murdered, there's a race for the prize, the beautiful widow and her lovely millions. They go together. Whoever wins Felicity Santana gets his fingers on the jackpot. The favourite, of course, is Bill Isaacs. He's the boss of this place now, and the natural successor to Peter Santana. He's got the power, but not the money. Then there's glamour boy, Hector Munro, every woman's dream workout. He's got the looks but not the brains. And then there's Oliver Razzle, the jumped-up call boy who simply fancies his chances because in one of those early Santana spectaculars made about Egypt a few hundred years ago, in a scene where Felicity was supposed to be Queen Nefertiti bathing in the altogether, in ass's milk, in a close-up he got to hold a palm leaf in a strategic position on her, from a wire off camera. He was so electrified by the proximity of her that the palm leaf quivered unceasingly throughout the shot. I'm afraid the memory of the palm leaf and all it symbolized to him has gone to his head. He's far too immature to take on Felicity. She'd eat him alive but he can't read the signs.'

Angel nodded and said, 'And where do you stand in this race, as you call it?'

Fairchild blew out a non-existent flame. 'I'm a non-runner, Inspector.'

Angel forced a smile. 'Maybe. Maybe. So you won't have any difficulty telling me where you were on Monday from around 7p.m. through to the early hours of Tuesday morning, the time Santana was murdered?'

'Don't look at me, Inspector. I was here in this caravan or on the set until about 11.30 or so that night. I suppose I reached The Feathers Hotel before midnight. I would be fast asleep by half past.'

Angel rubbed his chin. 'Can anybody confirm your arrival at the hotel? And that you stayed in your room all night?'

Fairchild frowned and stared at him. 'The night porter, I suppose.'

'That, I'm afraid, is not a conclusive alibi.'

Fairchild shrugged. 'It's the best I can offer.'

'And would you have any ideas as to why a dead pig was found in his bed?'

'Dressed in a pretty pink nightdress, I hear,' he said with a grin.

Angel looked at him and waited.

'I haven't the remotest idea, Inspector,' he said, then added mischievously, 'It takes all sorts.'

Angel heard a mobile phone ring out. It sounded like Vivaldi being played down a drain. Angel sniffed.

Fairchild dived into his pocket, opened the mouthpiece, pressed a button and spoke into it. 'Yes? … All right.' He closed the phone and looked across at Angel. 'I'm wanted on the set. You will have to excuse me.'

CHAPTER 9

It was four o'clock.

Angel was sitting in a small office. At the other side of a small desk was Oliver Razzle.

'Do you know anything about a loaded handgun being found in the gentleman's washroom here?'

Razzle's eyes grew bigger. 'A handgun? No. Certainly not.'

'Have you ever seen a gun anywhere in the studio complex?'

'No, Inspector. What's a handgun doing here? Whose was it? Was it lost?'

'People who own guns don't lose them, Mr Razzle. Do you know anybody here who owned one?'

'No. Frankly, Inspector, I'm very surprised. Do you think that someone here is a target? Do you think that whoever murdered Peter Santana is after somebody else?'

'I don't know, but Mr Santana died by being shot with a handgun.'

Razzle nodded.

Angel said: 'Where were you on Monday night, the night Peter Santana was murdered?'

'I was here, on the studio floor, until around 11.30. The scene was a bit tricky. We were using real sky as a backdrop and clouds kept rolling across it. We could more easily have used back projection, but Bill Isaacs wouldn't have it. He wanted the real thing.'

'Where were you after 11.30?"

'Straight home and straight to bed. It had been a long and tedious day.'

'Somebody can confirm that you were with them all night, can they?'

Razzle pulled a face that told Angel they could not.

'My wife was away that night,' Razzle said. 'Went up to town, London, on a Christmas-present-buying trip. She incorporated a visit to her mother in Dulwich, and an old friend. We used to live there, you know. She came back yesterday.'

Angel's eyes narrowed. There was another prospect without an alibi.

'Any idea why Mr Santana was murdered?' Angel said.

'No. None. I expect it was for money, but it doesn't make sense.'

Angel nodded. 'How did you get along with Mr Santana?'

'Fine. Just fine. I didn't see much of him, Inspector. He was in a different world really. Only came here for an hour or so a month, with his PA. Spent most of the time with Bill Isaacs. Occasionally called in Hector Munro or Samson Fairchild for a few minutes to iron something out. Or some big moneyman from a studio down south or occasionally from the US or from Rome or anywhere, he would see by arrangement, of course. If I saw a helicopter land on the pad at the other side of the car park, I knew that some big wheel was arriving and that Mr Santana would be in his office.'

'But you had met him? He knew you?'

'Oh yes. Of course. If we met in a corridor, or wherever, he'd stop briefly and shake hands. He'd say, "How's things going then, Oliver?" And I'd say, "Fine, thank you, Mr Santana," and then he'd smile and that was it. Somebody would jump in and say that he ought to leave and they'd rush off. It was always like that.'

'And what was he really like? He was seventy-two, wasn't he?'

'Well, lately, he was a bit thinner, a bit pastier and maybe his voice wasn't as strong, but he seemed just as vital and full of enthusiasm as he had always been.'

'And how did you get on with Mrs Santana?'

Razzle's eyes glowed. 'I have worked here for fifteen years, and I have known Felicity for about that length of time. I was a gofer then. Her gofer. She was a bit difficult at first. Rude. Ill mannered. In fact, she was downright nasty. But I persisted. I took all she doled out and she gradually came round. Eventually she began to like me. I got to like her. I found out that it was difficult to look at her, particularly close up, and not be affected by her beauty. She must have the highest cheekbones in the world. Her ears are like bone china. And she is so dainty. Tiny even. Like a porcelain doll.'

Angel had to agree but he didn't say so.

'Confidentially, Inspector, I have done more things for Felicity than her dresser,' Razzle said. 'And I have certainly *seen* as much,' he added with a concentrated gaze.

Angel's eyebrows came down with curiosity but he didn't ask.

'That was before she married Peter Santana,' Razzle continued. 'She worked here frequently. That's how they met. They got married ten years ago, you know. In the days when Mr Santana directed everything he wrote. He worked a lot faster than Bill Isaacs. He knew what he wanted and so did everybody else. There was no need for production meetings. Everything was smoother and faster.'

'And would you have any idea why a dead pig was found in his bed?'

'I heard that, Inspector. Strange. I hoped he wasn't going loopy or anything like that. I thought about it when I read it. And I immediately wondered what Felicity would have thought when she found out. The world could think he had some sort of unhealthy perversion going. And that would be an insult to her, wouldn't it?'

Angel shrugged. It was somewhat convoluted but he knew what he meant.

'Thank you very much, Mr Razzle,' Angel said.

'Oh?' he said, looking surprised and disappointed. 'Is that all you wanted to ask me?'

'For now, yes,' he said, getting to his feet. 'Can you direct me to Mr Isaacs' office?'

'Come in. Come in, Inspector,' William Isaacs said loudly in an accent from the backstreets of Chicago. He was short, balding and had a head compressed into his body like a frog. He had a lit cigar in his hand, and walked up and down as he spoke, slapping his feet down like flippers and waving his hands around using the cigar as a pointer. 'Sit down. Sit down. I'll tell you what I'm going to do with you, Inspector – What did you say your name was? Angel, that was it. Heck of a strange name for a policeman, I daresay. Hey, you're not that police inspector who always gets his man, are you? The one with the unbroken record of solving murders. Is that you? Must be. Well, what do you know? There can't be *two* men who are both police inspectors and both called Angel, can there? Is it *really* you?'

Angel shrugged slightly, nodded, hesitated then said, 'I suppose it is, yes.'

Isaacs smiled. 'Well, what do you know? I'll tell you what I'm going to do with you, Inspector. What's your Christian name? Michael, that's it. Don't mind if I call you Michael, do you? Here's what we're going to do. Why don't you ask me all you want to ask about Peter Santana here, right now. And then, dammit, then when you've done, my chauffeur can take us down to The Feathers for a steak dinner with all the trimmings. We can open a bottle or two of imported champagne and make a night of it. Just the two of us. All on me. A sort of pre-Christmas celebration on meeting each other for the first time, eh? You being a famous detective and me being a … a film director. What do you say to that, Michael?' he said, standing and leaning over the desk and holding the cigar in mid-air.

Angel was surprised by the energetic outburst from this American who must have thought that that was the way to deal with the British police when you had a murder case in your own backyard.

It was difficult for Angel to conceal his feelings. He wasn't the slightest bit interested in something for nothing. He wasn't on the take and never would be, and he would much rather be at home with Mary than lording it about in a hotel with Isaacs or anybody else. He had no desire to be in the man's company any longer than was necessary, either with or without champagne.

'That's not necessary at all, sir, thank you. I can ask the questions and be on my way in a very few minutes, I hope, all being well.'

The American saw that he had misjudged Angel's style. 'All right, Michael,' he said. 'Whatever *you* say. Fire away. Whatever you want.' Then he sat down behind the big desk and puffed on the cigar.

Angel said, 'Just a few questions.'

'Anything you want, Michael.'

'A loaded handgun was found in the washroom in the Sound Stage 2 building.'

Isaacs' eyes bulged out. He jumped up. 'What?' he bawled. 'I've been working in that building all day.'

'Do you know anything about it?'

'I should say I do not, Michael. I do not. Who found it?'

'Samson Fairchild.'

'Good man, Samson. Sound as a dollar, Michael. If he says he found it, he *found* it.'

'But you know nothing about it?'

'Absolutely nothing.'

'Can you tell me where you were on Monday from around 7 p.m. through to the early hours of Tuesday morning, the time Peter Santana was murdered?'

'Count me out, Michael,' he said with a grin. 'I was here directing Peter's latest film up to about midnight then my man took me home. I went straight to bed, slept through until the morning. Then was back here at my usual time, eight o'clock.'

'And you have witnesses that can confirm that you were with them all that time, I suppose?'

'Oh yes.'

'You're married?'

'Yes. Well, no,' he said. 'Well … sort of?' he said with a distasteful look that tightened up his craggy face.

Angel looked at him and frowned. 'So you were alone throughout the night?'

Isaacs transferred the cigar to his left hand, to stroke his chin with his right. 'It's like this, Michael. My wife has a mother living in Chicago. She ain't too well. She's over there … been there two years … making arrangements to have the old lady looked after professionally, you know. I don't know when she's coming back. I have a live-in housekeeper, Michael. Miss Mimi Johnson. All on the up and up, you understand. Her own room, quarters, bathroom, TV and everything. She was in the house all night. My driver delivered me home, brought in my briefcase, set the alarm and went home.'

Angel nodded. 'I shall need to know the housekeeper's and your driver's names and addresses.'

'That's all right. Miss Johnson lives in my house, of course. But I want you to know that it is all on the up and up.' He reached into the drawer and took out a card. He wrote something on the back and then handed it to him. 'There's my home address. Phone number. Mimi's there all the time except when she's down the market, which come to think is a helluva lot of the time. My driver is called Albert Broome. I've written his address on the back. All right?'

Angel pocketed the card. 'Thank you.'

Isaacs said, 'Now is there anything else, Michael?'

'A couple of things. You knew Peter Santana pretty well, didn't you?'

'As well as anybody, I suppose.'

'What was he like?'

'Well, he was a nice guy. Yes. The last couple of years he left most everything here to me … I was running the day-to-day business of translating his ideas into film. He was the ideas man, and they were damned good ideas. He was naturally a solitary person, Inspector. Spent many hours on his own developing the most original and outstanding plots. Didn't see many people … didn't want to see people. He experimented with just about every emotion the soul can encounter. He made a fortune for himself, and now for Felicity, and he allowed me to show off my talents as a director, and I picked up a few dollars on the way, which wasn't too bad. He will be sadly missed, I can tell you.'

'But was he a cold man?'

'Certainly not. If you mean in relation to Felicity – hell, no. He p'raps wouldn't get no Oscars for his performances in the bedroom, I don't know about that, but he was seventy-two, and she knew his age when she married him. I daresay it was no great love match, but it made a lot of headlines ten years ago, and did both their careers no harm at all.'

'Would you say Peter Santana was right in the head?'

'Absolutely. There never was a saner man. Throughout all his fantastic storylines, he always had his feet squarely on the ground. We had business meetings in his office in this building every month or so, and you couldn't get a shrewder hard nut than Peter Santana. And I come a pretty hard bastard too, I can tell you.'

'You had arguments?'

'All the time. But we'd thrash our differences out there and then. Peter was usually right and usually won. Should I worry? Whichever *one* of us was right made us *both* money. And we'd end up the best of friends. There was not a gram of vanity in either of us. Together we were a money-making machine. It is sad to see it is now in the past.'

'You don't think his age affected his thinking processes?'

'It sure did. It made him more mature. More sensitive. He became more aware of his mortality. Not in a morbid way, but in a matter-of-fact way.'

'So would you have any idea why a dead pig was found in his bed?'

'No. But I expect that it was to do with working out a plot he had in mind.'

'He didn't talk about a plot with a pig in a nightdress in a bed with you?'

'He never talked about plots and storylines in their early stages. We talked plenty about how scenes were to be interpreted *after* the screenplay was completed. He always had very fixed ideas about that. But the origination was strictly Santana's, and we stuck to it like it was holy writ.'

Angel sighed and stood up. 'Thank you very much.'

Isaacs stared at him. 'Is that it? Don't you want to ask me anything else?'

'Probably. But that's all for now.'

Isaacs jumped up. 'Are you sure there's nothing I can do for you, Michael?'

'You'll be seeing a lot more of me, I assure you.'

'If I can help you … if there's anything you need.'

'Yes. As a matter of fact there is something else.'

He opened his arms wide and said: 'Name it. Just name it.'

'Can you organize a pass for me so that I don't have to wrestle with the gorilla on the gate every time I have to come in here?'

'Is *that* all?'

It was 0828 hours on Monday morning when Angel arrived in his office. It had not been a satisfying weekend. He had taken home the armful of paper files containing the printouts from Peter Santana's three computers from 15 November up to 15 December, the day he had died. He had steeled himself to read every word during his spare time on Saturday and Sunday. It was mostly boring, unedifying work, made less bearable by Mary's many interruptions, mostly questions about Christmas. She had asked him who had sent them cards and who hadn't, about the fairy on top of the tree looking a bit dingy, about the arrangements for meeting his nephews and their wives before the big day, and then invited his opinion as to whether a turkey joint from Morrisons would be as good or better than one from Tescos. On the latter question, after some discussion, it was decided that it would be best to take a look at Sainsbury's before a firm decision was made.

Later that day, she had left the house to undertake various shopping jobs and had returned two hours later with a turkey joint bought from Marks and Spencer.

Angel loved Christmas, but the domestic arrangements preceding the great day he found rather tedious and endless. He was glad to get away from them that Monday morning and return to the business of solving crimes.

He put the bundle of files on the corner of his desk, threw off his coat and settled down in front of a pile of envelopes fresh in that morning.

He appreciated that Scrivens had done an excellent job in reporting a précis of what Santana had written during the last very industrious month of his life. He had missed nothing important. The only items Angel had extracted from the files that had any bearing on the investigation, as far as he could see, were that Santana had thoughts about setting up a trust which required the partial rewriting of his will, and the only reference to any dead pig was in the short incongruous list, which appeared in isolation in Santana's notes.

ether
cotton wool
dead pig fresh 100 lbs
silk nightdress
Monday night next

He gazed at the list again. It seemed to him to be associated notes related to some specialized operation, which presumably Santana had planned to take place on 'Monday night next'. The evening before or the day that he died. Whilst the last three items were directly associated with the actual murder scene, the first two items could not as yet be reconciled to anything at all. There had been no signs of the ether or the cotton wool at the murder scene, or indeed anywhere else. Santana surely didn't plan to organize his own death in conjunction with somebody else? The ether to make him unconscious? No. He quickly dismissed the thought. Santana's writings in no way depicted a man ready to leave this life. His stories – however extreme – ended full of optimism, with healthy ideals, good overcoming evil, the baddy being condemned to something horrible and the goody sailing off with the girl into the sunset, or some similar ethic.

There was a knock at the door.

He looked up. 'Come in.'

It was Scrivens. He was carrying a plastic bag bulging with tennis balls.

'Where do you want these putting, sir? And you were going to tell me about the scam that Laurence Smith was into, you said, when you had time.'

Angel frowned. He didn't like being accosted in that way. 'Not just now, lad. I'm up to my eyes. And I've got a job for you. Take those balls out. I don't want them littering up my office. Dammit, it's small enough.'

Scrivens' mouth opened. He wasn't pleased either. 'They're bunging up my locker, sir.'

'Well, I can't do with them in here. Take them out and come back here – smartish.'

Scrivens went out and Ahmed, seeing the door open, came in. 'Good morning, sir. Can I have a word?'

'What is it?'

'You know that cuckoo clock that you bought for only £10?'

'Yes, lad. What about it?'

'I took my mother to Leeds on Saturday to do some Christmas shopping, and they're all over the shops there at £120.'

'*All* over the shops?' he said. He didn't like exaggerated generalizations.

'Well, at least three different places, sir. Allbright's and Brown, Tompkins and that supermarket Cheapo's.'

Angel licked his bottom lip. 'The identical same clock?'

'I haven't seen any others, sir,' Ahmed said as he took a small scrap of paper out of his pocket. 'Anyway, I wrote the make down as I knew you would want to know.' He unrolled the paper and read: 'The Tikka Tokka Cuckoo Clock Company, Reebur, Suisse.'

That was the one.

Angel rubbed his chin. He couldn't understand the massive difference in the price and £120 did seem more realistic. 'Can you leave that paper?'

Ahmed smiled and put it on the desk.

'Ta,' Angel said.

Ahmed turned to leave.

'Just a minute. I've a little job for you.'

He gave the young man his car keys, told him briefly about Fairchild's fingerprints being on a gin bottle in a paper bag securely wedged between the spare wheel and a safety red triangle sign in his boot. He instructed him how to handle the bottle without smudging or adding his prints to it, and told him to bring it into his office.

Then he phoned Don Taylor, told him about the gun and the prints, which he would get Ahmed to bring up to his office forthwith. He asked him to check urgently if that was the gun that was used to murder Santana, and also to see if there were anybody else's prints besides those on the bottle or the gun.

Taylor said that he would deal with it straightaway.

Angel replaced the phone.

He leaned back in the chair. He was thinking that he could do with a bigger team. He recalled that he had sent Ron Gawber to search into the background of the clockmakers; he wondered when he might return. He liked to have Gawber at his side, particularly when a case was difficult.

He felt in his pocket for the card William Isaacs had given to him on Friday afternoon last. He took it out, looked at it, turned it over then turned it back again. From the back he copied Albert Broome's name and address on to a used envelope.

A few moments passed and Scrivens arrived.

'Come in, lad. Shut the door. Sit down. I want you to look this man up, Albert Broome.' He gave him the envelope. 'He drives for the big noise at the studio, William Isaacs. Isaacs says he took him home about midnight, the night Santana was murdered. That's part of Isaacs' alibi. Check it out. And see if you can find out what sort of a relationship Broome has with Isaacs' housekeeper, Mimi Johnson.'

'Right, sir.'

CHAPTER 10

The BMW slowed as Angel braked at the black wrought-iron gates of the Mansion House on Creesforth Road. He pointed the bonnet of the car between them and down the long winding drive cut through a big lawn and curtain of evergreen trees and bushes planted to mask the big house from the road.

He climbed out of the car, made his way up the four steps to the front door and pressed the bell.

A tall, skinny, blonde woman of about fifty, wearing a skimpy bright yellow dress, an ugly large-flowered apron and slippers, answered the door.

She smiled when she saw Angel, who introduced himself and showed his warrant card.

'Yes, I'm Mimi Johnson,' she said. 'Do come in. Please go straight through that door. That's the lounge. Please sit down … anywhere you like.'

'Thank you.'

She followed him in, tugging at the apron fastening as she walked.

There was plenty of choice of where to sit. It was a huge room with four outsize sofas and twenty or more large easy chairs arranged in circular groups of four or six around low coffee tables.

He chose the nearest easy chair.

Mimi Johnson disposed of the apron behind a chair with the dexterity of a magician and sat opposite him.

'It must be ever so exciting being in the police force,' she said, pushing her lips forward then turning them into a smile.

Angel smiled to save the embarrassment of answering.

'Would you like a cup of coffee … or anything, Inspector?' she said, with a long, lingering smile.

'No, thank you, Mrs Johnson.'

'You can call me Mimi. Everybody does.'

'Thank you,' he said quickly. 'I want to ask you about the whereabouts of Mr Isaacs last Monday night, the fifteenth.'

'Oh yes. That was the night Mr Santana was murdered and William, Mr Isaacs, worked late, to catch the natural moonlight, wasn't it?'

Angel nodded.

'Well, that's easy,' she said, running her hands down her waist and legs, ostensibly to straighten her dress.

Angel didn't notice. All he wanted were the facts.

'He got back here about midnight,' she said. 'Albert brought him in. That's his driver. Took his briefcase into the study … what he calls the den … then he left. William – Mr Isaacs – said he was too much awake to go straight to sleep. He would do some work in the study. I said I would make him something to eat. He said no. I offered to make him a milk drink. He said no to that too. I hung around for a while. He stayed in the study and had a few slugs of whisky … he calls it bourbon. He didn't know that I knew, but I heard him pouring it. He was irritable. I went in to see if I could do anything to help settle him down. I asked him what was wrong. He said it was work. It wasn't going right. I suggested that he took one of his sleeping pills. He told me to mind my own business. I said that he shouldn't drink so much, that the whisky would keep him awake. He didn't like that either. He bawled and shouted at me, because I questioned what he was doing. Then he got another glass and poured some whisky into it, about half full. He told me it was good for me, to drink it and go to bed. He knows I enjoy the occasional drink, but not neat whisky and not that much, nor to drink it in a hurry like that. It wasn't like him. Anyway, at first I refused, but with him, it's easier to do as he says. He went on and on about it, so I said if I could add some soda to it, I would drink it. So he let me fetch some from the bar in the dining room, then I drank it in front of him and went to bed. Funnily enough, I was soon asleep, and that's the last I knew until my alarm went off at seven o'clock next morning. I got up straightaway. He doesn't like to be late. Albert always picks him up at ten to eight. I went to his room about a quarter past seven with a beaker of tea. I had to waken him. He hadn't heard his alarm or it hadn't gone off. He was still irritable because he thought he was going to be late. But it was all right. Albert called as usual on time, at ten to eight, and I had him ready for him. I expect he got there on time. And that's about all I know.'

Angel nodded. 'What time did you say you fell asleep?'

'It must have been about one o'clock or a few minutes after.'

'So you cannot say for certain that Mr Isaacs was here from that time until seven o'clock on Tuesday morning, can you?'

Her mouth dropped open. 'Yes, he was. Where would he be?'

'If you were asleep you wouldn't know, would you?'

She looked confused. She put her hand to her face. 'Well, I don't suppose—'

'Does Mr Isaacs drive?'

'Yes. He has a new Chevrolet in the garage. Takes it out for a run most Sundays.'

Angel screwed up his face. He wasn't pleased. The alibi was useless. There were so many suspects in this case.

'I phoned the Swiss police in Geneva,' Gawber said. 'They speak very good English, I'm glad to say. They have passed the query down the line over there, and a few minutes ago, this email arrived.'

Angel took it and read it.

Re your inquiry – Tikka Tokka Cuckoo Clock Company, Mingenstrasse, Reebur. Local Polis report reputable clockmakers, established in 1866. Recently expanded into new factory in small industrial site in Reebur. Employing around 60 persons. Owner is mayor of village. Highly reputable. Wouldn't expect the company to be involved in anything criminal. Pleased to have been of service. Josef Schikerlan, Assistant Commander of Polis, Geneva.

Angel lowered the paper and looked up at Gawber. 'Well, that seems pretty conclusive.'

Gawber nodded. 'Where do we go from here, sir?'

'I don't know,' Angel said as he ran a hand through his hair. 'Why is there a roomful of cuckoo clocks for sale in that antique shop at £10 a time when they must cost more than double that to make?'

'There's a "For Sale" sign up on those premises, sir. Maybe they're reducing their prices to get shot?'

'Who would buy a roomful of one particular clock anyway? It's only a little shop in a backwater, not a high-street supermarket with a footfall of thousands.'

The phone rang. It was Taylor from the SOCO office. He had some information on the Walther. Angel was all ears.

'An attempt had been made to file off the registration number, sir,' Taylor said. 'I have managed to bring it back with a drop of the old nitric. It was one of a batch of forty sold by the makers to the Dutch police in 1970. It turned up in England in the hands of a villain in 1978 who has since served his time and is now dead. It was secured with four other handguns in a Royal Army Ordnance Corps depot in North Yorkshire, but that was broken into and this gun stolen from there in 1980 and there the record of it ends.'

Angel frowned. That wasn't much help. 'Was it the one that murdered Peter Santana?'

'Looks like it, sir.'

Angel breathed more deeply. Here was progress, at last.

Taylor said, 'There were seven rounds in the cartridge. It holds eight, so presumably the one round that had been spent had been the one that killed Peter Santana. There are no fingerprints on the rounds. But there are prints on the barrel, the trigger guard, almost everywhere else. They all match the prints on the gin bottle.'

Angel's jaw tightened. That was the news he didn't want to hear.

Taylor said: 'I'll put those prints on record, sir, if you want. I'll need the name of the man.'

'Samson Fairchild,' Angel said. 'He was the one who says he found the gun. They are his prints on the bottle.'

Taylor's voice changed. It was higher and he spoke quickly.

'Samson Fairchild, the film star?' he said. '*The* Samson Fairchild?'

Angel wrinkled his nose.

'I shouldn't think there's anybody else in the country with a name as poncey as that.'

'What's he like, sir? Have you met him?' he said quickly.

'He's got two legs and one head, lad, what do you think?'

Gawber looked across at Angel with eyebrows raised.

Taylor said, 'I'd like his autograph. For my daughter.'

'If he murdered Peter Santana, that's about all he could give you. In the meantime, did you find out anything else from the gun?'

'Yes, sir. You'll like this. I found specks of a powder here and there in the nooks and crannies on the gun, as if it has been left uncovered while powder had been applied to the face or the body. I thought it was flour at first but there's no gluten in it and it's tinted with carmine, I think, so it is very likely face powder. I could identify it positively if you could get a specimen for comparison.'

Angel's face lit up. His brain jumped about like the ball bouncing round the electric bagatelle board in the screws' recreation room at Strangeways. He replaced the handset in the cradle, still keeping his hand on it. He looked across at Gawber and said, 'Must get in touch with Trevor Crisp right away.'

He tapped in Crisp's mobile number. Of course there was no reply. He was working, but Angel was soon through to his voicemail. 'It's Angel. This is urgent, lad. Call me on my mobile, ASAP.'

He replaced the receiver, stood up, looked across at Gawber and said, 'Come on, Ron. Let's sort those cuckoo clocks out.'

They made for the door and Angel opened it as Scrivens was poised to tap on it from the outside.

'What you doing there, lad?' Angel said.

'I was coming to report on that chauffeur chap, Albert Broome, sir,' Scrivens said.

'Aye. Well, what about him?' Angel said, holding the door. 'Did he drop Isaacs at his house on Creesforth Road at about midnight on Monday the fifteenth or didn't he?'

'Yes, sir, he did.'

'And did he pick him up at 7.50 the following morning, Tuesday?'

'Yes, sir.'

Angel shrugged. He looked at Gawber and then turned back to Scrivens. 'Then there it is. In normal circumstances a perfect alibi. Except that Isaacs can drive, he has a perfectly good car in the garage at his house and he could have dosed his housekeeper with a tranquilizer and a stiff measure of whisky that would have made her sleep a good six hours. He could have shot Peter Santana easily, returned home and nobody's the wiser.'

Scrivens blinked. 'I didn't know that, sir.'

'No, lad, I know. I didn't. Did Broome drive him anywhere else at all that day?'

'No. He says he just took him back to his house at five o'clock that evening. That's all.'

'Anything else?'

'You asked me about his relationship with Isaacs' housekeeper, Mimi Johnson.'

'Yes. What you got?'

'He sniggered when I asked him what he thought about her.'

'Broome's young, is he?'

'About twenty-eight, sir. And he's happily married to a very pretty young woman – I've seen her – and they've got two kids. I shouldn't think he's at all interested in this Mimi Johnson. I pressed him further and he said that he believed his boss and Mimi had something going. He said that on one occasion he'd caught her and William Isaacs at it in the drawing room. Also that some Saturday nights, he drove them out to a hotel in north Derbyshire where they had a meal and more than a few drinks, and then played hanky-panky in the car as he took them back to Creesforth Road.'

Angel frowned and wrinkled his nose. 'I've got the idea,' he snapped. 'That'll do. Thanks very much, lad.' He didn't *want* to linger over the scene. 'But don't go away. There's something else you can assist DS Gawber and me with. Grab a roll of that broad plain parcel tape from the stationery cupboard and join us at the front of the station in my car, smartish.'

Angel stopped the car outside the antique shop. The 'For Sale' board was still across the window. The old fashioned doorbell rang as Angel opened the door. The three policemen went inside.

Juanita Freedman appeared from behind the counter, where she had a single-bar electric fire warming her feet.

Angel noticed that there were empty spaces in the window and around the shelves and walls of where stock had been sold and nothing had been put in its place.

There was still a cuckoo clock on the wall where one had been before when he had called. And it still had a ticket marked £10.

Juanita Freedman looked surprised and ill at ease at seeing the three men. She recognized Angel and flashed a quick welcoming smile.

He introduced her to Gawber and Scrivens and got straight down to business.

'I see you're still selling the cuckoo clocks at £10, Miss Freedman?'

'I'm trying to, Inspector. Still selling a few, but after a very good start, sales seem to have dropped off. I may have to consider advertising them in the *Bromersley Chronicle*.'

'How many did you have originally?'

'Two hundred and fifty.'

Angel looked at Gawber and indicated the room at the back with the door open. It still seemed to be crowded with boxes of cuckoo clocks.

He turned back to Miss Freedman. 'And how many have you left now?'

'All those. About a hundred, I guess.'

'Do you mind if we take a closer look at them?' he said, edging behind the counter towards the storeroom door.

She frowned. 'Not at all. Please go inside.'

Gawber and Scrivens closed up behind Angel.

The room had a big packing table in the middle. That was partly covered with the boxes and there were many of the same underneath. He selected six boxes at random and pushed two each at Gawber and Scrivens and kept two for himself. He turned to Juanita Freedman and said, 'As part of our ongoing investigations, we're going to open these six boxes. You will be here, witness to whatever we find.'

She shrugged. 'Yes. All right, Inspector. As far as I know, they have cuckoo clocks inside them. I don't know what you expect to find.'

Angel didn't reply.

The three men opened the boxes, which were securely sealed with an excess of brown sticky tape. It took a little while to cut through the tape and pull back the flaps. Each man took the actual clock out of the wrapping and removed the cardboard frame from the inside. They looked inside the back of the clock and around the cogs and wheels inside. They examined the weights, which were in separate partitions, then checked that the cardboard box had no false bottom or unnecessary packing to it. They checked everything there was in front of them, but could find nothing untoward.

At length, Gawber and Scrivens looked at Angel and he looked back at them. 'Right,' he said. 'Pack them back up.' He then turned to Miss Juanita Freedman and said, 'Who ordered all these clocks in the first place? And I'd like to see the invoice?'

'Inspector Angel,' she said, 'Mr Makepiece ordered them, I think. It was probably the very last item he bought before he died.'

Angel looked across at her with eyebrows raised. 'Mr Makepiece?'

She looked downwards and closed her eyes briefly.

'I'm sorry, Miss Freedman. You were fond of Mr Makepiece? He died naturally, I assume.'

'Oh yes,' she said. 'He owned these premises. He was a lovely man. This shop was his life. That's why it's for sale now. I am only helping out his solicitor … to close the estate. Lovely man. I used to assist Mr Makepiece sometimes.… It was originally on a casual basis … then as he became ill, I would come down part-time. He taught me a lot, and I was a good listener and I had a good memory. Once he'd given me the salient points about a picture or a piece of furniture, I would remember it. When a potential customer came in, I repeated it.… It made me sound most knowledgeable.'

Angel's mobile rang.

'Excuse me,' he said. He pulled out the phone and looked at the LCD. It was Crisp. He turned away, pressed the button, strode quickly out of the storeroom and through the shop towards the shop door to afford himself some privacy. 'Yes, lad?' he whispered.

'You left a message, sir?'

'Yes, Trevor. Listen. You've got to get a sample of Felicity Santana's face powder.'

Angel heard him gasp. 'What?' Crisp said.

'It's imperative. That gun has flecks of powder on it. It might be hers. If it is her face powder, we've got her for possession. Now I expect you would find her compact in her handbag. SOCO only need a few flecks.'

Crisp sighed. 'She's watched by everybody in the place, sir. She's a big number here, you know. And the only time she would leave her handbag would be when she's rehearsing and actually filming. And that's also when I'm doing my job, on a sound boom, only feet away from her. I don't see how I could ever get near her bag.'

Angel bit his bottom lip. He could see the problem. 'What about your girlfriend? I assume you've linked up with Felicity's gofer?'

Crisp took a second or two to reply. 'Well, er ...'

Angel's grip on the phone tightened. 'That's what your brief was. You *are* making progress there, lad, aren't you?'

'Oh yes, sir. It's just that ... I just don't want to jeopardize the relationship I have with her, for the sake of a sample of face powder.'

Angel wasn't pleased. The muscles round his jaw tightened. 'It's extremely important, lad. What's that girl's name?'

'Marianne Cooper.'

'Well, can't you tell Marianne Cooper that a cosmetics company is considering making an approach to Felicity about fronting a TV campaign provided that she already uses their product, and a sample would tell them that?'

Crisp didn't say anything.

Angel continued: 'You could polish that tale up, make it sound believable, couldn't you?'

There was more hesitation.

Angel's knuckles whitened. 'What's the matter, lad?'

'It's difficult, sir.'

'I know it's difficult,' he roared. 'If it was easy, you'd get paid six quid an hour to dole out revolting chicken and chips to kids that were even more revolting. Instead you get more than double that and you have a proper job … taking risks, making decisions, and generally making life better and safer for everybody else. Anyway, time's running out, see what you can do, and ring me back when you've the opportunity, *today*. Otherwise I will have no option but to come in there and take a sample from her formally and that would give the whole game away. The people there would close ranks and we might never find out who murdered Peter Santana.'

Angel closed the phone and thrust it in his pocket. He stormed back across the shop, shaking his head and pushing his hand through his hair. He would rather not have pushed Crisp so hard but there was nothing else to be done. That gun in the studio didn't simply arrive from nowhere. It belonged to somebody and it had been taken there for some reason.

CHAPTER 11

They arrived back at the station; Angel bustled up the green corridor, Gawber and Scrivens following.

Scrivens peeled off to the CID office.

With a sideways shake of the head, Angel indicated to Gawber to join him in his office. He pointed to a chair, closed the door, took off his raincoat, threw it at the hook on the stationery cupboard door, missed, looked at it, grunted, left it there and slumped into the swivel chair behind his desk, rubbing his chin.

His face was as long as a stick of rhubarb. After a moment's silence, he said: 'That gun found in the studio loo was used by the killer to murder Peter Santana.'

Gawber nodded.

Angel continued: 'If the powder found on the gun is found to be Felicity Santana's, what the hell does it prove?'

'Possession. That's five years, sir.'

'Aye, but what's the use of that? We're after finding a murderer, not a woman known to have been in possession.'

Gawber pursed his lips. 'Maybe there was to be *another* victim.'

'Who?'

'I don't know, sir.'

'We could maybe protect them, if we knew who they were.'

There was another silence.

'Felicity will get all Santana's millions,' Angel said. 'The trust Santana was thinking about setting up never happened, so she cops for the lot. If she had waited a few days, the trust might have been set up and she would have got half.'

'That's still a lot of cabbage, sir,' Gawber said.

Angel smiled. 'Rich folk always have to have more, on the basis that the poor don't know how to spend it. They fritter it away on food and clothes and rent.'

'Who would have benefited from the trust?'

'Up-and-coming writers … new writers with screenplays for original films.'

'Nobody else?'

'It was a way of filling the gap left by his death. Introducing new writing talent for after he had gone. It could have ensured a continuity of good screenplays for the studio that may have provided them with guaranteed work and earnings. Theoretically a very sensible idea. But the money to set up the trust would have come out of the big pot that Felicity has now inherited.'

'So she would be the only one possibly *not* to like the idea of a trust.'

'I think so,' Angel said wryly.

The phone rang. He reached out for it and heard a wheezy intake of breath through the earpiece. It was Harker. 'This Doonan murder – you've got a Laurence Smith in the frame for it, haven't you?'

'He's a possibility, sir,' Angel said.

'Is that all?' Harker said.

Angel frowned. 'He has a long-standing motive, sir, a record of robbery and GBH and ABH, and no alibi. He's been picked out from a suitably blanked-off photo from our rogues' gallery on a laptop by the man who served him in the pub. But we have nothing else on him. Can't make anything stick. We've searched his house. Only a load of tennis balls. He's into that old scam. Hardly anything to hold him on.'

'He's been spotted by a plain clothes officer from West Yorkshire police at Leeds/Bradford airport. He's radioed it in and their super has kindly passed it on. How kind of them. They are looking for somebody else. Their officer reports that a man who looks like Smith is waiting to board a plane to Zurich with two very big suitcases.'

Angel's eyes bounced. His pulse began to race again. Smith's nerve had gone and he was doing a runner, was Angel's first thought. 'Right, sir,' he said. 'I'll get straight on to it.' He banged down the phone. He looked quickly in the police telephone directory for the airport police, found the number and rang it.

He gave his name and rank and briefly explained his interest in Smith and asked for the time of the next plane to Zurich.

'There's one due in the air at 11.25,' the sergeant said. 'Flight 12A to Zurich. It's 11.20 now. It will already have been called.'

Angel licked his lips. 'Do you think you could find out if a chap called Laurence Smith is definitely on that flight, without arousing his suspicion?'

'I'll have a go, sir. Hold on.'

Angel heard some chatter, some electronic noise and distorted speech on a radio system followed by silence.

He turned to Gawber, who had picked up most of what was happening. 'Smith, possibly doing a runner to Zurich with two big suitcases,' Angel said. 'You might as well crack on with something else.'

Gawber stood up, nodded and said, 'What is he up to? He's not going to Frankfurt to get on a transatlantic flight to Rio de Janiero or Montevideo or somewhere else in South America, is he? If he is, we'll never catch him.'

Angel shrugged.

Gawber said: 'If I had committed murder, I suppose I would be prepared to travel that far rather than go to prison for twenty years.'

Angel nodded in agreement. 'Ask Ahmed to come in, will you?'

'Right, sir,' he said. He went out of the office and closed the door.

Angel continued holding on the phone for what seemed ages. At last he heard some more electronic chatter and the police sergeant came back and said, 'I've checked with immigration. It is a Laurence Smith, sir, about six feet two, black hair, long pasty face.'

Angel's heart jumped. 'That's him,' he said.

'Yes. He's on board, sir. The plane's just taxiing down to the runway.'

'Thanks very much,' Angel said, his pulse racing. 'How long is the flight to Zurich these days?'

'About an hour.'

'Thank you.'

He replaced the phone, immediately consulted the police telephone directory and found the appropriate Interpol office number. He soon got diplomatic clearance then found the number for the border guard at Zurich international airport, which he rang. The officer at Zurich international airport readily agreed to look out for Smith on Flight 12A from Leeds/Bradford, and Angel instructed Ahmed to email his photograph and description promptly to the Swiss immigration office there. The Swiss officer agreed not to approach or arrest Smith, but to try to find out his intended destination and to phone Angel back as soon as he had any information.

Angel replaced the phone, leaned back in the chair and sighed. After a few moments, he began fingering the paperwork and post that had been dropped on his desk that morning. There was a standard form from Bromersley magistrates clerk's office to the chief constable advising that an application for a licence to sell alcohol on premises not hitherto used for that purpose had been received, and the chief was required to approve or object to the granting of the licence. If the police objected, they were, of course, required to give their reasons, which would be considered by the magistrates and if contested would be heard in open court. The custom was that the chief constable canvassed his senior police officers' opinion, who usually raised no objection if the applicants were 'not known' to them and appeared to be suitably responsible people.

Angel glanced at it. He blinked when his eyes alighted on the name of the applicant: it was Liam Quigley. He read on.

The site of the proposed shop was the property previously known as the Antique Shop, Bull's Foot Railway Arches, Wath Road, and Liam Quigley was also recorded on the form as the owner of the freehold.

Angel rubbed his chin. This was a surprise. He slowly put the form back in its envelope and put it into his inside pocket. The fact that Liam Quigley now apparently owned the shop property and the flat above it might throw an entirely new light upon the relationship between Quigley and Juanita Freedman. He resolved to look into it just as soon as he could leave the telephone.

Angel looked at his watch. Zurich had only rung off five minutes ago. He stood up and began walking round the little office. He couldn't concentrate on anything else. It was worse than being at the Crown Court, waiting for a guilty verdict when you had a professional murderer on trial and a conviction depending on one shaky, nervous, dithering witness and no forensic on the prosecution side.

There was a knock at the door.

It was Ahmed. He saw that Angel was on his feet and sensed that all was not well. 'Cup of tea, sir?'

'What?'

'Would you like a cup of tea, sir?'

Angel looked round. His eyebrows went up. 'Yes. Thank you, lad. Two sugars.'

Ahmed frowned. 'You don't take sugar, sir.'

'I do today.'

The tea arrived, which Ahmed carefully placed on his desk. Angel was very thankful.

It was a further twenty minutes before anything at all happened.

Meanwhile he forgot about the tea and it was left to go cold.

The phone rang. Angel snatched up the handset. 'Inspector Angel, Bromersley police, UK.'

'It is Zurich airport police here. Your man, Laurence Smith, landed here twenty-five minutes ago. He was positively identified from your photograph sent by email. He went to the travel desk and bought a ticket to travel on the express coach from Zurich to Lugano, which leaves from the coach park opposite the Bahnhof Weidikon on the Birmendorferstraasse in the centre of the city at 1300 hours, and he is presently in a short queue for a taxi to take him there. Lugano is about 140 miles south towards the Italian border. It should take him just less than three hours.'

Angel wondered where on earth Smith was travelling to and how he could be further monitored. 'Hmm. Thank you. Do you know his actual destination?'

The officer hesitated. 'Lugano is the terminus, sir. Lugano, I suppose. It is a beautiful city, not far from the Italian border.'

Angel rubbed his chin. His eyes suddenly widened. He had an idea. 'Is there a place called Reebur on route?'

'Oh, where the big security printers is. Oh yes, sir, but of course?'

'What's that?'

'The big photo laboratory, and security printer, IMPRO. That's in Reebur, sir.'

Angel's eyes narrowed. 'I was thinking of the Tikka Tokka factory, where they make cuckoo clocks?'

He sensed that the officer was smiling. 'I don't know about that, sir. I suppose there could be some small factories besides IMPRO in Reebur. But Reebur is only a very, very small place in the mountains. IMPRO print sophisticated security documents and currency for banks, governments and businesses. They're very security conscious. I understand that you can't get near the place for security cameras, uniforms and passes.'

Angel felt his pulse begin to race; his mind was like a thousand ants in a thousand racing cars in the Monte Carlo Rally. Things began to fall into place. Of course, he thought! Laurence Smith is going to meet up with Harry Savage – an old buddy of his. They did jobs together. Stealing of copper wire from British Rail, for one.... Savage must have somehow got himself a job at IMPRO and is lining up a robbery or a swindle of some sort.

'I think I know Laurence Smith's ultimate destination,' he said to the Swiss policeman. 'Sounds like a possible threat against IMPRO. Would it be possible to contact the security chief there?'

'But of course. I expect I can look up IMPRO's chief security officer's phone number. You can approach him yourself direct, if you wish?'

'Thanks very much. Does he speak English?'

'I would think so. Most of us in the service are taught it in college.'

A few moments later, the officer reeled off the number. He even advised Angel of the international code from the UK. The two men then exchanged thanks and good wishes and rang off.

Angel immediately summoned Ahmed and told him to extract from the PNC the photograph and full description of Harry Savage and hold them ready, then he tapped out the telephone number of the chief security officer at IMPRO, who, much to Angel's relief, also spoke excellent English. His name was Paul Muller, and he was most concerned on hearing Angel's suggestion that Harry Savage may have infiltrated their sophisticated security systems and that with at least one other English villain, he might be considering some sort of crime against the security printing firm.

'I would be most interested to have a photograph and description of this Harry Savage, Inspector,' Muller said. 'If you email it straightaway, I will make immediate inquiries and ring you back.'

Angel thanked him, replaced the phone in its cradle, dashed through to CID, instructed Ahmed to send the photograph by email attachment, then returned to his office to wait.

More waiting.

Angel leaned back in the chair and licked his lips thoughtfully.

After a few moments, there was a knock at the door. It was Gawber.

'Just passing, sir. How's it going?'

Angel was pleased to see him. He brought him up to date and then said, 'Harry Savage's brother-in-law is Liam Quigley, isn't he?'

Gawber nodded. 'Are you wondering if in some way he is involved with this IMPRO, sir?'

'Just a thought. But even the three of them together haven't the brains to take on an outfit of that calibre.'

'Not the brains, sir. Maybe the brawn.'

Angel was considering Gawber's observation when the phone rang.

His face brightened as he reached out for it. 'Inspector Angel, Bromersley police, UK.'

It was Muller. 'I have checked off your photograph of Harry Savage against all my staff, Inspector, and I am pleased to say that he is not in our employment, Inspector Angel, in any capacity, nor has he ever been.'

Angel wrinkled his nose.

Muller seemed to make the statement with annoying triumphalism. Then he added, 'You seem to have been sent on zee wild duck chase.'

Angel pursed his lips. He didn't know what to say. He couldn't even be bothered to point out that the correct phrase was 'a wild *goose* chase'. It was true that he had allowed guesswork to override the facts but he couldn't think of any other likely reason why a crook like Laurence Smith, friend of Harry Savage, would be on a coach passing by Reebur.

But then he suddenly had another thought.

'You may be right, Mr Muller,' he said. 'Would you bear with me? Isn't there a factory there in Reebur called the Tikka Tokka Cuckoo Clock Company?'

'But, of course,' Muller said, sounding surprised. 'It is only a small factory next door. Reebur is only a very small village, Inspector.'

'*Next door*!' Angel yelled. He could not contain his excitement. He thanked Mr Muller kindly for his trouble and replaced the phone in its cradle. He turned to Gawber. 'Pass me that cuckoo clock box on that chair, Ron. I want the phone number on the label.'

Gawber read off the number and Angel tapped in the number on the phone pad. It was soon ringing out. He turned back to Gawber. 'Tell Ahmed to stand by. Hopefully, I'll want him to email that photograph and description of Harry Savage to the Tikka Tokka Cuckoo Clock Company.'

Angel was soon connected and was speaking to the proprietor, a Mr Meyer, who quickly grasped the situation. Ahmed promptly sent the email and in minutes Meyer phoned back to say that the photograph was indeed that of a Harry Savage who worked at the factory as a caretaker.

Angel's pulse took off again.

'He seems to be a very good employee, Inspector,' Meyer added. 'He has been with us six weeks now. He has no access to our lists of customers, their account details or any cash. He simply works around the factory pushing a trolley, collecting up the stuff for the waste bin, such as sawdust, wood shavings, wrapping paper, shredded paper from the office and waste from the canteen; he then takes it to the boiler room in the basement where he sorts it. Anything at all that is private or sensitive is burned in an incinerator with the waste from the printers next door, under the supervision of one of their managers.'

Angel nodded. There it was. That was the prize. 'Supervision or not, Mr Meyer, I believe that something valuable, that could be maybe copied or printed from, has been stolen by Savage from IMPRO's waste.'

'Do you really think so, Inspector?'

'I'm sure of it. I believe that whatever was stolen was then packed in and among a consignment of 250 cuckoo clocks of yours, which you innocently sent to Savage's partner and brother-in-law, Quigley, to an antique shop address that he had access to, here in Bromersley, in the UK. And that subsequently, with a bit of scheming – computers are so sophisticated these days – he has managed to produce images good enough to be used to forge passable Euros.'

'Oh dear. I know nothing about this, Inspector,' Meyer said.

'No, sir,' Angel said. 'I don't believe that you do.'

'What do you want me to do now?'

'Do nothing, Mr Meyer. Do not arouse Savage's suspicions. Let him complete his day's work for you without arousing his suspicions. But don't expect him to turn in for work in the morning. There is another villain, Laurence Smith, suspected of murder, who is also a friend of Harry Savage on his way to visit him, I believe.'

'Oh dear,' Meyer said. 'I don't want any trouble.'

'Don't worry. Through Interpol, I hope to arrange the arrest of both of them, hopefully in the next few hours.'

He asked Meyer for the address he had for Savage, which was at one of the few small houses in Reebur, thanked him for the information and cooperation and replaced the phone.

Angel turned to Gawber, who smiled.

'A couple more phone calls,' Angel said, 'and I think we can say that we have them safely in the bag.'

'What are you charging Smith with, sir? We know he must have murdered Vincent Doonan, but we don't actually have any evidence against him, do we?'

'He had those tennis balls in his possession, didn't he? That's evidence. Suspicion that he's working that old scam will be enough to pull him in and hold him.'

Gawber's eyes flashed. 'From Switzerland?' he said.

'From Swaziland, if necessary,' Angel replied heavily. 'By the way,' he added, 'I hope your passport is in order. Looks like there's a trip to Lugano likely for you and Ted Scrivens tomorrow.'

Gawber smiled. 'Oh? Right, sir.'

Angel reached out for the phone.

CHAPTER 12

It was at 10.25 p.m. on Monday night that Angel received a call on his mobile from the chief of police, Lugano, reporting that Savage and Smith were secure in separate cells in the police station there, having been arrested together by a squad of armed Swiss guard. The two villains were interrupted drinking wine and watching a video with two local girls in a rented luxury climber's chalet in the mountains in Reebur.

Less than six hours later, Gawber and Scrivens left for Lugano police station via Leeds/Bradford airport and expected to return with their prisoners later that same day if the flights departed and arrived on time.

Angel was delighted that he was at last making some progress on a case, and he went to the antique shop that morning with a light heart. He stopped the BMW outside the shop, where he duly observed that the 'For Sale' sign had been taken down from across the front of the building. He floated into the shop, feeling as carefree as Fred Astaire dancing up the staircase to paradise.

There were some answers he urgently needed from Juanita Freedman and Liam Quigley before he could sew the case up and pass it over to the CPS.

He pushed open the shop door, causing the bell to clang.

Miss Juanita Freedman was behind the counter. She had been hanging delicate glass decorations on a small Christmas tree by the till. On hearing the bell, she looked up, saw that it was Angel, frowned then changed it into a polite smile.

As he approached the counter, he observed that there were many more gaps in the stock than there had been on his previous visit, and reasoned that things must be going well.

'Good morning, Inspector Angel,' Miss Freedman said as she put the lid on the empty bauble box and pushed it under the counter.

'Good morning.'

'I am surprised to see you back so soon,' she said. 'Doing some last-minute Christmas shopping?'

He pursed his lips. 'No. Just tidying up a few loose ends, Miss Freedman. The shop has been sold, I see,' he said, glancing back in the general direction of where the sign had been.

Her eyes glistened. 'Yes,' she said, smiling. 'Liam Quigley has bought it. Isn't that great? It means that I will be able to stay here. It is such a relief.'

It was the first time he had seen her look happy. He was pleased for her. 'It had been a worry, had it … *where* you were going to live after Mr Makepiece died?' he said thoughtfully, licking his lower lip.

'A serious worry, Inspector. I doubt if I could have afforded to pay the rent for any modern flat even if I could have found one. When Mr Makepiece was alive, this flat was part of my remuneration and of course it was useful to him, me living above the shop. I could lock up and attend to everything when he was away on holiday or business. He used to be away a lot, attending auctions and sales. Of course, those were the good days,' she said with a faraway smile.

Angel rubbed his chin. He had that awful feeling that she was in for a fall. 'And what does Liam Quigley intend doing with it now?' he said. 'Has he discussed it with you?'

'Oh yes. It will pretty well stay as it is,' she said. 'Liam says he won't be stocking as many antiques, though. More like curios, fast-selling lines like these cuckoo clocks. They were just a start. He's looking round now to see what other unusual novelties he might buy.'

Angel bit his bottom lip for a few seconds, then he said: 'Did you know that he had applied for a licence to retail alcohol from these premises?'

'No,' she said. 'I was not aware of that.'

'I am afraid so.'

She was momentarily stunned. 'You mean convert this shop into an off-licence?'

He nodded.

She narrowed her eyes, then lifted up her head, stretched her neck, took a deep breath, made herself as tall as she could and said, 'I'm sorry, Inspector, I don't believe you.'

He wasn't surprised at her reaction. He reached into his inside pocket for the envelope from the magistrates clerk's office addressed to the chief constable; he took the letter out of the envelope, unfolded it and passed it to her.

She looked at him then at the letter, which she took reluctantly. She read it, then read it again. Her face slowly drained of all colour. Saying nothing, she pushed the letter back at him. Then her eyes flashed and she lunged out at the Christmas tree on the counter and sent it flying across the shop, the glass baubles splintering into pieces.

Angel stood there. He hardly seemed to notice.

She put her hands up to her face then said: 'I think I knew it all along. He wants the flat for Sonya. He was always looking for a place for her … so that he knew where she was … so that he could keep an eye on her. He'll put her in here as manager. That was his plan all along. I have no idea where I will go.'

'How do you know he doesn't want you to stay? You could run the shop for him. Better than his daughter could. Besides, it might take more than one person.'

She shook her head, the corners of her mouth turned downwards. 'No. He wants the flat for *her*. Anyway, I can't see me handing out six-packs all day, Inspector. My heart wouldn't be in it. No. All good things come to an end. I should have realized that when Mr Makepiece died.'

'And Liam Quigley may not get the licence from the magistrates. They are not keen on granting licences to people with a police record, and his record will certainly be made known to them.'

She shook her head. 'It's too late, Inspector. I will have to face up to it. There is nothing here for me. I shall have to leave. I can't live in a state of uncertainty any longer.'

Angel frowned at this. He thought a moment and then said: 'There is something else, Miss Freedman. Something I haven't yet told you.'

She looked at him closely.

'It's almost certain that he won't be granted a licence, because I will shortly be bringing a case against him for forgery,' he said.

She frowned, shook her head and said, 'Forgery?'

'Yes,' Angel said.

She stared ahead into nothingness, her face blank; she was finding it difficult to believe what she had heard.

'He has a printing press somewhere,' he said.

'Oh?' she said, hardly hearing what he was saying.

'Do you ever hear a machine running? Is there anywhere where he could carry out such an operation?'

'I don't know of anywhere.'

'Didn't Sonya Quigley take you out to a pub one night – last Thursday night if I remember correctly – and you didn't get back until after eleven o'clock?'

Miss Freedman came out of the fog, narrowed her eyes and said: '*She* told you *that*? I thought that was just a … just a spontaneous night out.'

He looked straight into her eyes. 'I'm sorry, Miss Freedman, she said that her father gave her £40 for you and her to have a good time,' Angel said. 'To give you a good time, to keep you out for four hours at least and not to let you get back here before eleven o'clock. There would be a reason for that.'

'I can't think what. But I'm beyond being surprised at anything you tell me now about him.'

'Because he wanted to do something in here or in your flat that he didn't want you to know about.'

'Like what?'

'Like bringing in a printing press, and operating it. It would have made some noise; there would have been some vibration. It would have roused your curiosity.'

'He couldn't get in my flat so it must have been down here.'

'Is there anywhere in this shop where he could set up a press that he wouldn't want you to know about it? Is there another room beyond that storeroom?'

'No. Just the loo,' she said. Then her jaw dropped. 'There's the cellar! There is a trapdoor in the stockroom floor that leads to some steps down into the cellar. We used to store stuff down there when we were short of room, but it's rather damp.'

Angel's eyes shone with excitement. 'That'll be it. Show me.'

They rushed into the storeroom to a place near the farthest wall behind the table where the boxes of cuckoo clocks were stacked.

'Under there,' she said and began clearing the boxes. Angel piled them on to the table and pushed them anywhere they would go. The area was soon cleared and she pointed down at two metal rings, each secured to a bolt in the wooden floor. The rings were only about eight inches apart and each rested in a depression specifically made for them so that when they were not in use, they would lie flat and could be safely walked over. Angel reached down and grabbed hold of one of them, lifted it out of its position and yanked it up. The trap door came up easier than he had thought. It was hinged and revealed a black hole below about a yard square. He went to the other and pulled that open. He could now see some stone steps and a handrail.

Juanita Freedman pressed a switch on a panel of switches on the wall in the storeroom and the cellar flooded into light.

Angel climbed down the steep, stone steps. He stood on the flagged cellar floor and took in the scene with some satisfaction. It was only a small, grimy, cobwebby space with a low ceiling, but big enough in which to set up four six-foot-long tables in the shape of a square. On the farthest table was something irregularly shaped, covered over with a grubby bed sheet. Next to it were reams of white paper and a hand guillotine. On the other two tables were piles and piles of banknotes. He reached over and took one of the notes from a pile. He looked at it, felt it and ran it through his fingers. He had to admit it looked and felt right. It was ten Euros. It was the right colour, red, and the picture of the architecture looked accurate, as far as he could remember. He held it up to the light and frowned. There was no watermark; no metal strip through it. He shook his head. He looked at the number, then he looked at the number of the notes on several other piles. They were all the same. He wrinkled his nose and then put the forged note in his pocket.

'Have you found it, Inspector? Is it a printing press?' he heard her call down.

He turned and made his way back up the steps. 'Yes. I am afraid it is, Miss Freedman. This is very serious. Liam Quigley is now a wanted man.'

Juanita Freedman slumped in a chair by the table. Angel looked at her. She was a changed woman. She seemed much older. 'How long will he get?'

'Well, the case has to be proved first,' he said, trying to let her down lightly.

'But there can be no doubt?'

'No. There's other supporting evidence. There's no doubt.'

'How long will he get?' she repeated.

'It's up to the judge, of course, but a minimum of four years, I would have thought.'

She lowered her head and stared at the floor.

'I'm sorry,' Angel said. 'You had a near squeak there with a nasty piece of work, Miss Freedman.'

He took out his mobile and tapped in a number. As it rang out he looked down at her and said, 'I think you'll find that it will have been for the best.'

There was a click and a voice said: 'CID office. PC Ahaz. How can I help you, sir?'

'Ahmed, I want you to ask DI Asquith if he can spare two men to bring Liam Quigley in to assist with inquiries in connection with the forging of foreign currency. I expect he'll be at his home address. Also I want you to ask DS Taylor if he'll bring his team urgently to a forger's den in the premises of the Antique Shop, Bull's Foot Railway Arches, Wath Road. It'll be mostly a matter of sweeping for fingerprints.'

'Right, sir,' he said brightly.

'You can tell Don Taylor I'll wait at the premises until his arrival.'

'Right, sir.'

He pocketed the phone. He looked down at Juanita Fredman. 'I'll be here a while,' he said.

She didn't reply.

'I think we should close the shop,' he said and he walked out of the storeroom, through the shop to the door, turned the open/closed sign round to show closed, then shot a bolt on the door across to the lintel. When he returned to the stockroom, Juanita Freedman was standing and trying to smile. 'Would you like a cup of tea while you're waiting, Inspector?'

Angel smiled.

'Good morning, sir.'

'Good morning, Ahmed. Has Liam Quigley quietened down?'

'Yes, sir. But he keeps asking for his solicitor.'

Angel wrinkled his nose. 'Aye. Well, he's entitled to see him. Will you tell him that Mr Bloomfield is on the premises and will be coming to see him today?'

'Right, sir,' Ahmed said.

'And what about Savage?'

'Nothing to report, sir. He's quiet enough. Says nothing. He's no trouble.'

'Has his solicitor been?'

'No, but he's been advised.'

'Hmm. It's early yet. Will you ask the duty jailer to take Laurence Smith into Interview Room Number One? Mr Bloomfield is already in there. They can have as much private time together as they need, but let me know when they are ready, will you?'

'Yes, sir,' Ahmed said.

'And will you see if you can get hold of Trevor Crisp on his mobile? It's Christmas Eve – I don't know how easy-going they are at that film studio. They might still be actually working there. If he isn't, tell him I want to see him in my office before he starts working his way towards the new year alcoholic haze. I should be free after about eleven.'

'Right, sir,' Ahmed said and dashed out of the office.

The phone rang. It was Don Taylor. His voice indicated that he was quite excited. 'There were stacks of Liam Quigley's fingerprints all over the printer, sir. They were on the forged notes, the guillotine and the outer wrapping of the paper, which had the watermark of a dove, and labels on the wrappers showed it was paper made by "Scrubb, Knight and Kelly" of County Cork, in Ireland.'

Angel smiled. 'That means we've got them both, Don. Will you let me have your report ASAP and let's get shot of it?'

'Right, sir.'

He replaced the phone.

There was a knock at the door. It was Gawber.

Angel looked up. 'Fully recovered from your winter break?' he said with a wry grin.

Gawber smiled.

'Did they give you any trouble?'

'Not with the cuffs on, they didn't, sir. Smith protested a lot at first. Unusual for him.'

'About what?'

'About the murder.'

Angel frowned and shook his head. 'I'm going to interview him shortly. I want you to sit in with me.'

'Is there any new evidence, sir?'

'No.'

Gawber's eyes narrowed.

Angel said: 'The good news is that Quigley's prints are all over the forger's den. And the special paper he used was stolen from a delivery lorry parked outside a transport café on the A1 near Scotch Corner in April. It was intended for security printers in Gateshead. We know that that job's down to Harry Savage. So that sews it up nicely, Ron. We've now got enough to support the charge of forgery by both Quigley and Savage to pass it over to the CPS.'

The phone rang. Angel glared at it. He reached out and snatched it up.

Before he could speak, a voice from the earpiece said, 'Come up here, smartish.' It was Harker. 'There's some matters I must speak to you about urgently,' he added. It was followed by a loud click, which made Angel pull a face of pain.

'I wish he wouldn't do that,' Angel said as he banged down the phone.

He turned to Gawber. 'It's the super. I've got to go. Start collating all the evidence against Quigley and Savage. Let's get that off to the CPS. I have no idea what the super wants, but I hope he doesn't keep me. I want to get to Laurence Smith. See if I can winkle out the truth.'

Gawber frowned. 'You mean a confession, sir?'

'I live in hope, Ron,' he said.

Gawber knew it was true.

Angel opened the office door.

He didn't yet have any hard evidence.

He charged up the corridor, knocked on Harker's office door and went in.

'Ah. Angel,' Harker said with a face like a nightmare.

The office smelled of camphor. On his desk, in addition to piles of files and heaps of paper, was a jar of Vick, plus a jug of water and a tumbler.

'Three of our cells are occupied and it's Christmas Eve,' Harker said. 'Don't you know what that means?'

Angel pursed his lips. 'They are all ex-convicted villains, sir. One of them is a murderer.'

'If you had delivered them there *yesterday*, they could have gone to court this morning and been remanded or … moved on …'

Angel's eyes flashed. 'You mean released, sir.'

'Or sent to the Crown Court.'

'Or been released,' Angel insisted.

Harker's red face went redder. 'Well, if the magistrates saw the evidence like that, then yes, released.'

Angel felt his stomach muscles tightening. 'All three have records, sir. I have cast-iron cases against two of them for forgery.'

'There you are. Those two could have been residing in Armley. But the point is that they are going to be in this station over Christmas, which means that I have to have a constable on jail duty, running about after them as if this was a hotel. That's a man less on public house roster.'

'Laurence Smith is being held on a tenuous thread, I admit, but he *is* suspected of murdering Doonan, sir.'

'There are Christmas dinners to organize. We are still a civilized country. We can't give prisoners takeaways at Christmas when they are still theoretically innocent and haven't been tried. We'd have civil rights wallahs round like flash bulbs at a public exhumation.'

'In the past, we have had Christmas dinners sent in from The Feathers, sir.'

Angel thought Harker's eyes were going to fall out and roll down on to the floor. 'I know all about that,' he bellowed. 'But look at the cost, lad. Look at the cost.'

Angel stood there, helplessly looking at the ugly, red-faced, skinny man in the ill-fitting suit, which he had heard was a gift from his mother-in-law after her husband had died two years previously.

He licked his lips patiently as Harker continued.

'You think policing is about catching murderers, don't you? But that's the glamorous side of policing. That's why *you* keep getting your name in the papers. That's why the press think *you're* so wonderful. They don't know how useless you are at organization, cost control and budget management. They don't know how much you have frittered away in air fares alone this week. Flights out to Switzerland, indeed! This place is getting more like Butlins every day. It should be a tightly run force, properly organized, controlled and budgeted. You always send my budget straight out of the window. I would not worry, but it is my direct responsibility to the chief constable.'

Angel blinked. It was some time since he'd had an onslaught like this from him. The only thing to do was to wait until it was over.

'What have you got to say for yourself?'

Angel rubbed his chin. 'Well, sir, I'm just doing my best to … to find the truth … and when someone is guilty to … to see that they are brought to court. That's all.'

'Yes. Yes. Yes. You've two murders in hand, haven't you? What's the progress on those?'

'I have a suspect for the murder of Doonan, sir. A Laurence Smith. Been through our hands before, robbery, GBH and ABH. At the moment, I can't make anything stick. He's been held on the tennis ball scam. Can't hold him much longer. I'm formally interviewing him again this morning.'

'I remember him. If you can't make a case, for God's sake let him go. That'll save us a few thousand.'

Angel's eyes flashed. 'He ran off to Switzerland to avoid arrest, sir. I've just had him brought back. He might run off to somewhere where we can't get at him.'

'The other case, the murdered millionaire film producer chap and the pig in the nightdress?'

Angel's face changed. 'There are too many suspects, sir. I don't know.'

'*You don't know*?' he screamed. 'You've got Crisp in there undercover, haven't you? Is he still in there?'

'Yes, sir.'

'Ridiculous. The newspaper boys are still having the time of their lives, making fools of us. I thought you were going to make a statement to shut them up.'

'The only thing that will shut them up is a full explanation, sir.'

'And you haven't got one, have you?'

'No, sir.'

Harker smiled.

Angel was concerned. He rarely saw him smile.

'I think this is the case that has you beat, lad,' Harker said.

Angel didn't reply. He was furious but he had learned it was better not to retaliate. It only gave Harker more ammunition. Besides, he could be right. At that moment, Angel hadn't a clue.

In an instant, Harker's smile disappeared. Something was wrong. He snatched at the middle desk drawer, pulled it open, found a small plastic bottle, unscrewed the top, shook out a pill, tilted back his head, threw the pill into his mouth and reached out for the glass of water. He took a sip and tried to swallow the pill. It wouldn't go down. He tried again. It refused to go. He tried again. Third time lucky, he swallowed the pill successfully, put the glass down in front of him and then seemed to realize that Angel was still there. 'Aye. Well, you'd better get back to it, lad.'

CHAPTER 13

Angel sat down at the table, pressed the record button and said: 'Interview of Laurence Smith. Present, Mr Bloomfield, DS Gawber and DI Angel. 1000 hours. 24 December 2008.'

Angel sat back in the chair. He suddenly became aware of a pain in his chest. It wasn't new to him. He'd had the pain many a time before. He first remembered it as a boy – then it was the result of eating a large piece of apple pie and rushing out to play football against a Jubilee Park wall. That was twenty-five years ago. He hoped it was the same pain. He tried to swallow it away, several times. Then he tried to burp. Neither worked. He really would have liked to have been on top form to take Smith through his paces.

He looked across the table. Everybody was looking at him. He'd have to begin.

'Mr Smith,' he said, 'why did you empty your bank account and fly off to join Harry Savage in Reebur?'

'I fancied Christmas in the Swiss mountains,' Smith said. 'Harry Savage is a friend of mine. He had invited me to stay with him for a holiday, that's all.'

'You were interviewed by me and conditionally released last Thursday, the eighteenth. The conditions were that you weren't to go into the Fisherman's Rest and you weren't to leave town.'

'Well, Mr Angel, I must have forgot. I didn't see any harm in it.'

'Did you tell anybody about your new address in Reebur?'

'No. Didn't see any reason to tell them.'

'Wasn't it because you wanted to disappear, and you didn't intend coming back?'

'No.'

'Isn't it true that you secretly ran away to Reebur with two suitcases packed with all your valuables to avoid being arrested for the murder of Vincent Doonan?'

'Definitely not. I didn't murder Vincent Doonan, and I didn't take all my valuables. I told you … it was just a holiday.'

'You took all your money and everything from your house that was worth anything, and you bought a single ticket, not a return.'

Smith wriggled awkwardly for a few seconds then shrugged. 'I didn't know how long I was going to be away.'

'Were you and Harry Savage planning another job out there?'

'Certainly not. I told you, it was just a holiday.'

'Didn't you and Harry Savage fall out with Doonan over the distribution of the cash proceeds from the sale of some copper wire the three of you had stolen from British Rail in 2001?'

Smith looked at Bloomfield and mouthed something meaningless to Angel. Bloomfield's eyebrows came down thoughtfully for a second then he nodded.

'Well, yes,' Smith said. 'But that was ancient history.'

'Wasn't Harry Savage pleased to see you?'

'I suppose he was. Yes.'

'Was he *very* pleased to see you?'

'Well, yes.'

'I would think so. Wasn't it because you had just shot dead your mutual enemy, Vincent Doonan?'

'Certainly not. That's a ridiculous thing to say.'

'Not *that* ridiculous. You were identified by the landlord, Clem Bailey, as the man who shot Vincent Doonan at the Fisherman's Rest a week last Tuesday evening.'

'Well, he must need glasses because it wasn't me.'

'But you can't say where you were.'

'I can, and I did. I told you, I was at home all evening and all night.'

'But you haven't a single witness to prove it. You could have been anywhere.'

'I don't *have* to prove it.'

Angel knew he was right. This wasn't getting him anywhere. The apple pie was still with him. He looked at Gawber, who he hoped was thinking of something useful to ask, but nothing came.

'How tall are you?' Angel said.

Smith blinked. 'Six foot two.'

'Would it surprise you to hear that all the customers in the Fisherman's Rest that we managed to trace said that the gunman who shot Vincent Doonan was over six feet tall?'

'There must be a million men in the country who are over six feet tall.'

'Aye, but none of them were identified as the murderer and also had a motive to murder Vincent Doonan.'

'Nevertheless, *I didn't do it*.'

There was a pause.

Gawber said: 'Where did you get the gun?'

'I didn't have a gun,' Smith said then his face changed. His eyes shone with anger. He looked up at Angel, then at Gawber and then at Bloomfield. 'You've no evidence against me. You're just fishing. Look, I know my rights. Now charge me, otherwise I'm walking. You can't stop me.'

Then he stood up quickly, nudging the table, causing it to judder and make a loud noise.

Mr Bloomfield pulled at his sleeve. 'Wait a minute, Mr Smith. Sit down. Don't make a disturbance. I'll ask for an immediate discharge. Sit down.'

Angel raised his head and looked at Gawber, who shook his head. Angel sighed. 'Very well, Mr Bloomfield, your client can go.'

Smith gasped. His arm shot up in the air, he clenched his fist and jerked it downward at the same time, letting out a very loud and decisive, 'Yes!'

Angel leaned over to the recording unit and said, 'Interview terminated 10.08.' And he switched it off. The pain in his chest felt like a brick. He sat back down in the chair and wiped his forehead with his handkerchief.

Everybody else made for the door.

Smith saw him and came back, sniggering. He nudged up against him and said, 'Don't I get an apology then, Inspector Angel?'

'Don't push your luck, lad.'

Angel heard Smith give a high-pitched giggle as he followed Bloomfield and Gawber out of the room.

He clenched his fists tightly under the table.

'Has Smith gone?'

'Yes, sir,' Gawber said, closing the office door. 'Can't believe his luck.'

'Nor can I. I think I'll have to have another good look through the evidence. There must be something I've overlooked.'

Gawber frowned and said, 'Trevor Crisp said that Doonan whispered in his dying breath that it was Liam Quigley who shot him, sir.'

'I hadn't forgotten, Ron. I hadn't forgotten. I had thought that that might have been deliberate spite on Doonan's part. Retaliation for Quigley's many accusations about him and Sonya. Doonan must have hated the man's guts. Also, it's possible, nay probable, that Doonan did not recognize his killer. He was so muffled up, nobody else in the pub could identify him. And Quigley has an alibi provided by a very assured Miss Freedman.'

'Didn't Clem Bailey identify the mugshot of Laurence Smith?' Gawber said.

'He only said he *thought* it might be him. That would not have counted as much in front of Mr Justice Fleming.'

He nodded. Judges never took anything as read, these days, particularly when the information was given by the police as prosecution witnesses.

'Another point, where did the murderer get the gun from?' Angel said. 'And what happened to it afterwards? Judges like to know these things. If they know what the actual weapon used was, and it is shown in court as an exhibit, they tend to smile on us.'

Suddenly they heard some running footsteps and giggling outside in the corridor.

Angel broke off and looked at his watch. 'What's that?'

Gawber said: 'I think it's Christmas hi-jinks, sir. Starting a bit early.'

Angel blinked. 'Oh yes. It's Christmas Eve.'

'Coming to the Fat Duck for a drink at lunchtime, sir?'

'Oh yes. But there are a few jobs I must do before then. Firstly I want to see Ahmed then I must see Trevor Crisp.'

Gawber stood up. 'If you've done with me, sir, I've some bits I want to finish off. I'll see if I can find Ahmed and send him in.'

'Thanks, Ron.'

Gawber went out. As the door opened there was more scampering and giggling. The door closed. Quietness returned to the office.

After a few minutes, there was a knock at the door. 'Come in.'

It was Ahmed.

'You wanted me, sir?'

'Yes, lad. I want you to get me the home phone number of a Mrs Makepiece. She's the widow of the owner of the antique shop down at Bull's Foot Railway Arches on Wath Road. I don't want the shop. I want her home address. I expect she lives in or near the town. The phone will likely still be in her husband's name.'

'Right, sir.'

'And you'll be joining the team for a drink at the Fat Duck at lunchtime, won't you?'

Ahmed smiled. 'Right, sir. Thank you. DS Crisp is here, sir.'

Angel's face brightened. 'Good.'

Angel went out and Crisp came in.

'Sit down, lad. Have they closed down the studio for Christmas, then?'

'Yes, sir. Some of the big wheels have already flown off to warmer climates. William Isaacs has gone to Chicago. Felicity Santana has gone to Barbados. Hector Munro has gone to some long-lost relations in Scotland. And Samson Fairchild has gone to … I can't remember where, somewhere warm.'

'You've had five days working there. I hope it's been worthwhile.'

'Yes, sir. And they've given me the sack and paid me £200 cash in hand, casual labour, the going rate for unskilled labour,' he said with a grin as he handed the wage packet over to him.

Angel took it, glanced at it and put it in the desk drawer.

'I've learned a lot about film-making, sir,' Crisp said and he pulled a small polythene bag out of his pocket and put it on the desk in front of Angel. 'And that's the sample of Felicity's face powder you wanted. It's smeared on to a tissue.'

Angel's eyes glowed. 'Ah,' he said, his eyebrows rising like the opening of London Bridge. He reached out for it. 'I won't ask you how you got it.'

'No. Don't, sir. I nearly got caught.'

Angel frowned as he picked up the phone. 'Felicity Santana doesn't suspect anything, does she?' he said.

'No, sir,' Crisp said. 'Marianne Cooper, her gofer, covered for me.'

Angel let out a small sigh and quickly tapped out a number.

The phone was answered straightaway. 'SOCO. DS Taylor.'

'Trevor Crisp has managed to get some face powder that might match the powder found on the Walther,' he said into the phone. 'I've got it here.'

'Ah.' Taylor sounded pleased. 'I'll send somebody down for it, sir. It won't take long to make the comparison.'

'Great stuff. Thanks, Don,' he said and replaced the phone.

'Mrs Santana is obviously playing it careful, sir. She gives nothing away in the studio. She is pretty well as rude and arrogant to everybody in equal measure, perhaps more so to Mr Isaacs.'

'He's her natural adversary.'

'Everybody else treats him like a god.'

Angel nodded. 'Who fits the profile, the characteristics, I gave you?'

'I have prepared a simple chart, sir,' he said, taking out his notebook. 'You said the murderer would be dishonest, ruthless, handsome, rich and probably older than her.'

Angel nodded.

'Well, sir, there have been four men hovering round her of late,' Crisp said, referring to his notebook. 'They are William Isaacs, Samson Fairchild, Hector Munro and Oliver Razzle.'

He stopped and looked at Angel.

'Go on, lad. I'm listening,' Angel said.

'Now, *William Isaacs* could have all those characteristics, sir, except that he is far from handsome. *Samson Fairchild* I suspect could be dishonest and ruthless. I suppose he's handsome. I don't know how rich he is. He is certainly older than her. *Hector Munro*: I don't know if he is dishonest or ruthless. He is certainly regarded as handsome. He appears to be rich, he's not been out of work since he started acting, and he would be a couple of years older than her. And *Oliver Razzle*.

I suspect he could be dishonest. Don't know about ruthless. Don't think he's rich enough for Felicity, and I think he must be about five years younger than her.'

Crisp stopped.

Angel waited a moment or two, rubbed his chin and said, 'Putting it like that, Trevor, it looks like there are two nominees: Samson Fairchild and Hector Munro.'

'That's how I see it, sir.'

There was a knock at the door.

Angel said: 'I expect it'll be a lad from SOCO, for that face powder sample.'

Crisp picked up the polythene bag, opened the door, exchanged a few words with the caller, handed the bag to him then returned to his chair.

'So if we could find out which one of them came by the gun, we would know who did it, even though we can't, at this stage, prove it,' Angel said.

Crisp nodded and was about to reply when the phone rang.

Angel reached out for it. It was the civilian on the switchboard.

'There's a Mr Love on the phone for you, sir. He's Irish, I think, and he sounds a bit rough. Will you speak to him?'

Angel breathed out a long sigh. Love couldn't have rung at a better time. 'I certainly will. Hold on just a moment, please,' he said, then he put his hand over the mouthpiece, turned to Crisp and said, 'Anything else pressing?

'No, sir.'

'Right, well, I'll see you at the Fat Duck at lunchtime?'

Crisp took the hint. 'Oh yes, sir,' he said, and he went out and closed the door.

Angel removed his hand from over the mouthpiece. 'Put Mr Love through, please.'

'Hello there, Mr Angel,' Mr Love began.

He was an Irishman of doubtful character, but he had helped Angel out of a tight corner a few times in the past and this couldn't have been a tighter one.

'I didn't see your message,' Love continued, 'because it wasn't there until Saturday night and I didn't get to reading the paper until a few minutes ago, and now it's Christmas Eve, wouldn't you know? I should have been on the ferry to see my dear mother over Christmas at St Joseph's in Balley Ocarey, but I haven't the necessary. And how can I be helping you, dear Mr Angel?'

'Mr Love, you may have heard I am investigating the murder of a film producer who was shot dead—'

'Surely now. It's all over the papers, isn't it, and him with a sow in a pretty silk nightdress snuggled next to him.'

'A Walther PPK/S was the murder weapon. I want to know who bought the gun.'

There was silence.

Angel said: 'Are you there?'

'Yes, I'm here, but I was tinkin', that's a really tall order yous giving me for a Christmas present, Mr Angel.'

'We have got it down to one of two suspects. All I'm wanting to know is which one.'

'Ah. Well, you know, you wouldn't like to give me the names of the two punters, would you?'

'No.'

Love wasn't a bit surprised. He had known Angel almost twenty years.

'But I can tell you a bit about the gun,' Angel said.

'Oh. Go on den. You never know, it might help.'

'Well, it has had a chequered career and an attempt had been made to file off its number. It was stolen with four other handguns from an RAOC depot in North Yorkshire in 1980, and it must have been sold to my suspect in the last few weeks or even days.'

'Hmm. 1980 is a long time ago, Mr Angel. I've lost and won a few punt on the harses since then. You wouldn't like to give me an advance in the way of encouragement, would you, Mr Angel?'

'No, Mr Love.'

'Oh dear, Mr Angel. Where is your Christian charity this Christmas?'

'Come and have a drink with me and my team at the Fat Duck. I shall be there in about half an hour.'

'No, tank you. The sound of handcuffs rubbing against webbing, the shiny black boots and the smell of Silvo, fair puts my teeth on edge.'

Angel smiled but said nothing.

'But I'll do what I can on the udder matter. But I tell you, I risk more than a good thrashing when I'm listening out about guns, Mr Angel. One day I have a fear a gun might be used on me. Now I must try and get home to Mudder. If I get anyting, I'll be in touch. Merry Christmas.'

'Merry Christmas,' Angel said mechanically and replaced the phone.

He wasn't pleased. He wrinkled his nose then sighed.

He knew he had to open all the doors and get help from wherever he could. Love didn't sound at all optimistic. Of course, it was in his interest to make the job sound as difficult and as dangerous as he possibly could. It pushed up the price.

There was a knock on the door. It was Don Taylor from SOCO. He had a smile on his face. 'I am pleased to tell you, sir, that the samples of specks of face powder on the gun that killed Peter Santana match the sample on that tissue taken from Felicity Santana's powder compact.'

Angel's eyebrows went up. That was welcome news. At least it confirmed that the Walther had been in her presence at some time in its very recent past; also that it therefore tended to suggest, as Angel had thought all along, that Felicity was a party to Peter Santana's murder.

'Ta, Don. Thank you very much.'

Angel and DI Asquith's teams congregated at the Fat Duck and had a modest Christmas drink, a pork pie and free black pudding on a cocktail stick.

Ron Gawber bemoaned the prospect of being closed in with his wife's relations for two whole days, while Ahmed indicated that he was enthusiastically looking forward to visits from several aunts and uncles and their offspring. Scrivens said that he was travelling up north to his parents and seemed pleased about it, while Trevor Crisp, wearing a big smile, drank rather too much, said very little and looked like a very contented man. Outside in the square, a brass contingent from the Salvation Army began to play 'Hark The Herald Angels Sing' and some of the team wandered out to the pub doorway to hear better and offer a contribution to the collecting tin.

The relaxed and informal chatter lasted for an hour or so, then the various members broke up and each made his way to their respective homes.

Mary had the house seasonally decorated, warm and cosy.

Angel had a nap in the chair in front of the King's Singers, then had tea while watching *The Great Escape* for the eighth time. Later, he got changed, and they went to church at 11.30, got back at one in the morning and went to bed.

Christmas came and went faster than two cascaras.

The Angels didn't do anything exciting. They snoozed; watched the same old films again. *The African Queen* came up again and Angel prompted Bogart to say his dialogue when he was late coming in on cue.

He had a pile of books he wanted to read, some crime stories, some biographies.

The weather was cold. The house was cosy. The nights were long. The food was good. The books mixed. The TV was rubbish....

CHAPTER 14

It was 0835 hours on Monday 29 December. The Christmas break must have been a successful and happy time for most of the force at Bromersley police station, as Angel could hear laughing and chattering as the staff traversed the CID corridor outside his office door.

Angel had called a crime case conference in the CID briefing room for 8.40 and was at his desk in his office preparing himself. He had instructed Ahmed to have A4-size photographs taken off the internet of all the persons involved in the Santana case stuck to the blackboard with their names in large print underneath.

Through the office window, he saw Trevor Crisp arriving late, in a red, noisy Lamborghini, scrambling out of the low-slung seat, slamming the door shut, as a dark-haired young woman waved to him and then drove the monster noisily away.

The team had assembled in the room early and had chosen the five seats at the front, nearest to the blackboard. There was DS Gawber, DS Crisp, DC Scrivens, PC Ahmed Ahaz and DS Taylor.

Angel arrived in the room at 0839 and closed the door.

'Dr Mac can't be with us,' he said, looking across at them. 'He's still away on his Christmas break, and I've asked

DS Taylor to sit in with us. Now, this Santana case is providing me with a great deal of bewilderment. You all know what was discovered up at the farmhouse.'

He then gave a quick précis of the personal background and circumstances of the Santanas and went through, item by item, each of the unusual discoveries made at the farmhouse on the day of the murder of Peter Santana.

Then he said, 'What some of you may not know is that the face powder found on the Walther was indeed the same powder that Felicity Santana uses. It was not known until Christmas Eve. It is likely, therefore, that the gun was on a dressing table, or a bed or somewhere, uncovered, as she was powdering her face.'

Taylor said: 'That doesn't mean, of course, that she is the only woman in the world using that particular face powder, sir.'

'That's true,' Angel said. 'But it would support the case against her, if we are able to mount one.'

Taylor nodded.

Angel then went on to confirm the conclusion made following Crisp's report on the time he had been working at the studio: that Santana had been murdered by one of two men, Hector Munro or Samson Fairchild.

'Common sense, logic and the facts point to them,' he said. 'They are both experienced actors. And you can't believe all the guff their agents put out about them.'

Nobody said anything.

Angel said, 'Has anybody any other ideas? That's what we're here for.'

'Where did the gun come from?' Gawber said.

'It must have been procured by one of the men,' Angel said. 'It would not have been easy for a woman to have negotiated with the likes of Jack "The Gun" Leary or any of that crowd. The face powder certainly indicates that it may have been some time in Felicity Santana's presence.'

'It was found in the washroom at the studio by Samson Fairchild,' Crisp said. 'I saw him find it.'

'Had you not thought it could have been a bit of acting to suggest his innocence?' Angel said.

'No, sir,' Crisp said. 'I thought it was the real thing. He's not that good an actor.'

Some of the gathering smiled.

'You might be right,' Angel said, looking at Crisp. 'That makes him a less likely suspect than Hector Munro, does it?'

'I wouldn't have said that, sir,' Crisp said, being very careful.

Angel's face creased. 'We are not getting far with this ...'

Scrivens said: 'Can I ask, sir, was a motive determined for the murder?'

'Money, lad,' Angel said. 'And, presumably the questionable luxury of being Felicity Santana's husband. Peter Santana is murdered. Leaves everything to his wife. Murderer marries her. The perfect mix of a beautiful woman and a shipload of money. There was some talk of Santana changing his will, so the murder was probably brought forward before any change was made.'

'The woman would have to be in love with the murderer then?'

Angel hesitated. 'That's the ... presumption, lad.'

Ahmed said: 'What's the pig in the silk nightdress got to do with it, sir?'

Angel sighed and ran his hand through his hair. 'I wish I knew, Ahmed. I only wish I knew.'

The team looked at each other, then at Angel expectantly.

After a few moments, Angel said, 'Right, if nobody has any bright ideas, we shall have to resort to old-fashioned legwork. There are no shortcuts. Those two men, Hector Munro and Samson Fairchild, from now on are to be treated as prime suspects.'

He looked at Crisp and said, 'When do they resume work at the studio, lad?'

'The studio opened first thing this morning, sir. Mr Isaacs will be there. He has to be there. Almost certainly Mrs Santana will be there. She's in nearly every scene. And

Samson Fairchild. I think scenes including them both were scheduled for today. But Mr Munro could be still away. He's not wanted until tomorrow.'

'Do you know where he lives?'

'He is renting that big house on Manchester Road. He'll be there or at the gym on Woodhall Street, I expect.'

'Right. Ahmed, get out all the info you can on Fairchild and Munro. You'll have to depend mostly on publicity guff from the studios, but see if you can dig deeper and find anything from newspaper cuttings or by researching their childhood and their parents and brothers and sisters.'

Ahmed nodded. 'Right, sir.'

'Trevor, I want you to give me a full report on Felicity Santana. I want to know everything about her. I mean *everything*. Her parents, past lovers, everything. Has she got her own teeth? What she eats and drinks. What she likes. Who she likes. Everything.'

Angel turned to Gawber and said, 'Let's go and see Munro.'

DS Taylor called out: 'Don't you want me to do something, sir?'

Angel turned and said, 'Yeah. Get that pig out of the deep-freeze, take it to a vet and ask him to give it a post mortem … what it died from. And see if there is anything at all unusual about it. Anything at all.'

Angel slowed the BMW outside the big house on Manchester Road; he pointed the bonnet through the iron gates round the big circle behind the bushes and up to the front of the house.

The two policemen got out of the car and made their way up the stone steps to the door. Gawber pressed the illuminated doorbell button.

There was a fifty per cent chance that the man who opened the door was the murderer of Peter Santana.

Angel's hands were shaking. His face was hot and in his chest was a food mixer revolving out of control and creating excessive vibration. He tried to contain himself by breathing in and out several times.

The door was eventually opened by a handsome, tanned young man with piercing blue eyes.

Angel held up his warrant card and said, 'Police. DI Angel and DS Gawber. Are you Mr Munro? Hector Munro?'

The man's eyes narrowed. 'I'm Hector Munro, yes.'

'We are investigating the murder of Peter Santana and I would like to ask you some questions. May we come in?'

Munro pulled the door open and stood well back behind it. 'Of course.'

He directed them to a room at the back of the house and when they were all seated, Angel began.

'Sorry to trouble you, Mr Munro. Just a few questions. Won't take long.'

'That's all right, Inspector. Please feel free to ask me whatever you wish.'

Angel nodded. 'You are very fond of Felicity Santana, aren't you?'

'Yes. Oh yes, but no more than most red-blooded men of my age, I suppose,' he said with a smile.

Angel noticed the lips and the teeth. He had heard that women were supposed to swoon at his smile. The smile, however, didn't do anything for him.

'But you are in closer proximity to her than most red-blooded men of your age,' Angel said, 'if you don't mind me returning the question to you like that.'

'Playing opposite her in several films, I suppose it's true.'

'Eight films, actually, Mr Munro,' Gawber said.

'Really?' Munro said. 'I hadn't realized it was as many as that. Time passes quickly when you're having fun. But … yes … well, I was … I am quite fond of her, yes.'

'And it is well known,' Angel said, 'that you dumped your last wife when you knew you were going to be playing opposite Mrs Santana again in this present film.'

Munro's face changed. His lips tightened. 'That was just *one* tabloid newspaper. I don't know where they got their information from. Nobody should take any notice of what they read in those scandal rags.'

'So there's no truth that you and your wife are going to be divorced, then, sir?'

'Er. Well, yes. We are in the stages of … But what has it to do with you, Inspector?'

'It could be said that you … set your cap at Mrs Santana.'

Munro frowned. 'Set my cap?'

'Excuse me,' Angel said. 'It's a northern expression. I'll rephrase it. It seems to me that you made a deliberate attempt to seduce Mrs Santana.'

'That's outrageous. Certainly not. Who says so?'

'Where were you between midnight on Monday night, 15 December, until one o'clock on the morning of the sixteenth?'

His eyes flashed. 'In bed, here, I should hope. Why?'

'Who with?' Angel said.

Munro's steely blue eyes shone with anger. 'By myself. Why?'

Angel sighed.

Munro added: 'That was the time Peter was murdered, I suppose.'

'Yes, sir,' Angel said.

Munro's tongue licked his top lip. 'Look here, this is getting ridiculous. I think I ought to get in touch with my solicitor.'

'I think you should.'

Munro leaped up and made for the door. 'I'll phone him now.'

Angel nodded. 'I suggest you ask him to meet you at the police station. I was about to ask you to accompany us there.'

Munro glared back at the two men. 'Won't be a minute,' he said, then he went out and slammed the door.

After a few moments Gawber said, 'What do you think?'

Angel shrugged then rubbed his chin. 'Could be our man, Ron, I suppose.'

Then they fell silent. The house was quiet. There was no sound of him making a call. They looked round the room. Eventually Angel looked at his watch. He seemed to have been gone a long time just to make a phone call. The two men looked at each other.

'You don't think he's done a bunk, sir?'

They heard the sound of a distant door banging.

Angel rushed to the room door, opened it and went into the hall. He was just in time to see Munro appear, running up some steps presumably from the basement. He pointed to a telephone on the table in front of them. 'I had to use the telephone in the kitchen. That one's not working.'

Angel said: 'Is everything arranged, Mr Munro? Is he meeting us at the station?'

'He'll be there in a quarter of an hour, Inspector,' Munro said, panting.

Angel said, 'Oh, a local man. Right. Let's go.' Then he marched down the hall to the front door, opened it and the three men went out and down the steps to the BMW.

Gawber showed Munro into the front seat next to Angel, and then got in the back.

Angel put the key in the ignition. Surprisingly, the car didn't start. The engine turned over vigorously enough then spluttered into nothingness. He tried this again with exactly the same result. Then twice more, producing even weaker responses.

Angel wrinkled his nose. 'Hmm. Never done this before. I'll ring Norman Mallin of traffic,' he said.

Munro undid the seatbelt and opened the car door. 'We can go in my Range Rover. We'll be there in no time. You can send your man to sort the BMW out when we get to the station, can't you? The car will be safe enough left in this drive.'

Angel wanted to get this man in the interview room ASAP. The idea sounded good to him. He nodded and withdrew the ignition key.

Munro got out and crossed the area in front of the house to a large garage door. He pulled a remote control from his pocket, pressed a button and the door began to rise. Inside was only one vehicle: a big, almost new Range Rover. He got into the driving seat and drove it up to the BMW. The two policemen then piled in the back seat and they were soon away.

Munro seemed happy. He switched on the radio and found some loud music. He pointed the Range Rover out through the gates of the drive and turned right towards the police station. He had only driven a little way when he pulled up at the side of the road near a narrow street corner outside a large house with a garden in front. He pulled on the handbrake. 'My throat's dry. There's a small shop round this corner where I can get some cough sweets that I like. Do you mind? Won't be a tick.'

He got out of the vehicle and rushed off, leaving the engine running and the radio blaring out.

Angel and Gawber watched the few vehicles pass them in both directions and noticed several pedestrians on the pavement looking at them disapprovingly, sitting in the back of the Range Rover with the raucous and loud music blaring out.

They knew it was against the law to have the engine running in an unattended vehicle on the highway.

Angel made a decision. He unfastened the seatbelt, eased himself forward, reached out between the front seats and switched off the ignition, which immediately silenced the engine, then he tried to find the radio controls. He did eventually find the off button and the screaming and the banging of drums stopped. He was pleased with the contrasting quietness and eased back into the seat.

Gawber smiled.

Then Angel heard something that sent a chill down his spine. It was the ticking of a clock. 'Get out, Ron. There's a bomb in here.'

'What?'

‘A bomb! Get out.’

Gawber also heard the ticking. His blood turned to ice. He struggled madly out of his seatbelt and they both tussled with the door handles. They were all fingers and thumbs. Angel eventually managed to open his door and got out on to the pavement. Gawber was still wrestling with the off side door handle. Angel leaned in and dragged him out on to the near side. They left the door open and dashed away along the pavement. They didn’t get far.

There was a mighty explosion.

As he ran, Angel was deafened, lifted off the pavement a few inches for about six feet, hit with something like an airborne car door, peppered with flying glass and landed hard on the pavement about twenty-five feet away from the car. He lay there, panting, face on his arm, his heart beating like a threshing machine. His ears hurting, wanting to burst, needles in the back of his neck, blood running down his cheek.

It was silent, eerie and frightening. He lay there for ages. His breathing was becoming steadier. Then suddenly he heard his mobile phone ring out. It was in his jacket pocket. He pulled a face. The ring persisted. Then he felt the touch of a hand on his shoulder.

‘Are you all right, old chap?’

Angel opened his eyes. He was being turned over by two men. ‘The ambulance is on its way,’ one man said.

He could hear. Thank God.

Angel eased himself up on one elbow to look round for Gawber. A small crowd had arrived. In the middle of them, he saw him. He was seated on a low wall about twenty yards further away. He was talking to a man and a woman. He was upright and alive. Angel sighed.

The mobile was still ringing. He fumbled into his pocket and pulled it out. He glanced at the LCD. It was Ahmed.

‘Yes, lad. What is it?’

Ahmed sounded relieved. ‘Oh, glad I caught you in time, sir. I wanted to warn you that Hector Munro could be dangerous. He has a record. Served four years in Barlinnie for safe-breaking when he was only eighteen. Changed his name to Munro. His father is Archie McGinney, head of the McGinney gang who blew up the Caledonian and Western Bank in Glasgow in 1999 and got away with twenty million. Now his father's doing twelve years in Durham.'

'Thank you, Ahmed,' Angel said. He smiled wryly, then he said, 'Now, listen up. This is extremely urgent. Ask DI Asquith, as a favour to me, to send three uniformed men immediately to Hector Munro's place on Manchester Road to arrest him.'

'Right, sir. On what charge?'

Angel eyes flashed. 'The attempted murder of two police officers, for starters,' he snapped. 'They'll have to move smartly. He won't be hanging around waiting for them. He's on the run.'

'Right, sir.'

Angel closed the phone then opened it and tapped in a number.

It was soon answered. 'DS Mallin, traffic division.'

'This is Michael Angel, Norman. My car won't start. The battery seems all right. I have had to leave it at the front of the big house on Manchester Road. Will you bring it in and sort it out?'

'Yes, sir.'

'Thanks, Norman.'

Angel heard two-tone sirens. He looked round as he closed the phone. An ambulance arrived. Its door were opened, the step lowered and two men dashed up to him with a stretcher.

'Now then, sir. Let's have a look at you. Tell me, where does it hurt?'

'I am all right. I can walk. Just let me stand up.'

CHAPTER 15

Angel was taken to hospital and kept in overnight. He was treated for shock, and had cuts from flying glass in the back of his neck cleaned and dressed. His hearing had corrected itself and he was almost back to normal. He wanted to return to work. But the hospital doctor, unknowingly supported by his wife Mary, had other ideas.

Ron Gawber had suffered similar shock and cuts to his neck and to one hand and had also been kept in hospital the one night for observation.

So it was two days later, at 8.15 a.m., the morning of New Year's Eve 2008, that Angel was collected from his home by a police car and delivered to the police station promptly at 8.28 a.m.

He smiled as he opened his office door, switched on the light and found everything just as he had left it (apart from the addition of more mail, reports and general bumf piled on the desk).

He took off his coat and hung it on the hook on the side of the stationery cupboard, then bounced into the chair and banged the arms to convince himself he was there. He liked that leather chair. He reached out to the radiator and touched it. To discover its customary warmth on that cold December day gave him even more satisfaction. He reached out for the phone and tapped in a number.

It was soon answered. It was Ahmed. There was pleasure and surprise in his voice. 'You're back, sir!'

'Yes, lad. Is there any tea going?'

'Won't take a minute, sir,' he said eagerly.

'Let it mash, Ahmed. Let it mash. Don't rush it. And is DS Crisp in there?'

'Er. No, sir.'

'When you see him, tell him I want him.'

'Right, sir.'

'Is Don Taylor in?'

'I think he's out at Hector Munro's house on Manchester Road, sir.'

'That's right, Ahmed. Thank you.'

Angel replaced the phone and it rang immediately.

'Norman Mallin, sir. I heard you were back. Your car is perfectly OK now. I'll drive it round and put it in your parking space.'

'Thank you very much, Norman. What was wrong with it? It's never let me down before.'

'It had a potato shoved up its exhaust.'

Angel blinked. 'Really? *That* old trick.'

He replaced the phone.

Crisp knocked on the door and came in. 'Great that you're back, sir.'

'Thank you, lad. Sit down. Who took over my court attendances while I was off?'

'I did, sir.'

'What happened exactly?'

'Savage and Quigley were remanded to Armley.'

'That was expected. What about Munro?'

'He was charged with the attempted murder of you and Ron Gawber. And he was remanded to Doncaster.'

Angel frowned. 'What about the charge of the murder of Peter Santana? Did you speak to Mr Twelvetrees at the CPS about that?'

'He wasn't a hundred per cent happy, sir,' Crisp said.

'I thought there was enough evidence to make the case stick. I spoke to Mr Twelvetrees at length from the hospital and gave him a verbatim account of the damning interview Ron and I had had at Munro's place on Monday, where he had no alibi and offered no defence.'

'I also spoke to him on Monday afternoon, sir, after you. He told me you had phoned, and when I told him all that background and name change and everything that Ahmed had dug up, he seemed impressed, but he still felt that it needed some forensic or something that would put Munro and Mrs Santana closer together. I think he wants a photograph or CCTV or half a dozen witnesses that saw them together in the act!'

Angel let out a long sigh. 'I thought it was all sewn up.'

There was a knock at the door.

'Come in.'

It was Ahmed with the tea and his notebook in his hand. He saw Crisp and said, 'There's somebody in reception for you, Sarge.'

Crisp looked at Angel, who sanctioned his departure with the nod of his head.

'Thanks, Ahmed,' Crisp said and he went out and closed the door.

Ahmed placed the cup and saucer safely on an old CD of 'BT and how to install Broadband', which Angel used as a coaster.

Angel sipped the tea eagerly and nodded appreciatively.

'I got a phone message for you, sir,' Ahmed said, holding up his notebook. 'Confidential, she said. Came in while you were off. Can I read it to you? My handwriting's not that great.'

Angel nodded. 'Who is it from?'

'It's from a Mrs Makepiece, sir,' he said. 'She sounded very nice. She said would I kindly tell Inspector Angel, you, that the matter he discussed with me in confidence has been dealt with satisfactorily? The matter now seems to be in first-class order, and she thanks the inspector very much indeed for his kind attention and for bringing this important matter to her notice.'

Angel held the cup from his lips briefly, looked at Ahmed and said, 'Right, thank you, lad. When I have finished this tea, I am going straight to the antique shop on the Bull's Foot Railway Arches.'

'Good morning, Miss Freedman.'

'Oh, Inspector Angel, you gave me such a shock. I wasn't expecting you.'

He pursed his lips. 'Really? I thought that you were. I believe you have something to tell me?'

Her eyebrows shot up. Her mouth dropped open. 'Good gracious, Inspector. How very strange. However did you know? Are you a … thought reader?'

'No. On the contrary, I'm a rather practical man. What's the matter?'

'Oh dear, Inspector. You were certainly in my thoughts. How very perceptive of you. You must have a gift. That must be why you have a reputation for always getting your man … In this case, your woman, I suppose. I was reading in the paper that you've never been beaten by a case yet. You've got quite a reputation.'

He pulled a face like a food taster at Strangeways. Every day he was convinced he was about to lose it.

'Yes. I was working round to coming to see you,' she said. 'I thought I could telephone you, but then that didn't seem right. There are some things that need saying face to face.'

'Indeed,' he said.

'I was probably going to telephone the police station this afternoon to make an appointment to see you.'

'Well, I'm here in person. You can say whatever it is straight out, can't you?'

'It's not easy, Inspector.' She swallowed. 'It is actually a confession.'

'I know.'

'You know? Oh dear. Will I get a long prison sentence, or …'

'Spit it out, lass,' Angel said.

She suddenly said, 'I told you a lie, Inspector. I had to. I told you that Liam Quigley came to my flat a week last Tuesday afternoon, at teatime, and spent the whole evening and night with me until eight o'clock the following morning. It was not true. He arrived at my flat that night at about a quarter to eleven. I have no idea where he was before then, but he wasn't with me.'

Angel looked up. 'Vincent Doonan was shot at nine o'clock. You provided an alibi for him.'

'I know *now*. I didn't know *then*.'

Angel sighed.

Twenty minutes later, Angel was back in his office in deep conversation with Gawber.

'So I want you to go down to the antique shop, and take another statement from her—'

Gawber wasn't pleased. 'What has made her change her mind, sir? She's not going to change it back again, is she?' he said. 'Are we going to book her for wasting police time?'

'No. It's not like that. You've got to feel sorry for her, Ron. She was very lowly paid by old Makepiece and was in dire straits. When he died, he owed her a small sum in back wages, but she couldn't bring herself to ask Mrs Makepiece for it. The debt was enough to put her behind with all her domestic bills. She was living hand to mouth. Quigley came along, promised to clear all her bills, put her employment at the shop on a proper footing and made other proposals not totally unwelcome, I suppose, to a woman in her position. I guessed that something was wrong, so I contacted Mrs Makepiece. She invited Miss Freedman to her house. They spent some of Christmas together … not a happy time for either of them, I'm sure. Mrs Makepiece has paid her the owed wage, cleared her debts and they have worked something out over the rent of the flat.'

'That alibi gone means Quigley shot Doonan,' Gawber said.

Angel nodded. 'It does.'

Gawber grinned. 'He'll not be buying the antique shop then.'

'It's no surprise that the building society wouldn't make the advance to him, either, so the sale has fallen through. Now Mrs Makepiece is working something out with Miss Freedman and they are talking about running the shop as an antique shop in partnership together.'

'That's great, sir.'

'So I want you to get that statement, drive over to Doncaster and formally charge Quigley with the murder of Doonan.'

Gawber smiled. 'Couldn't be a better way to end the old year, sir.'

Angel nodded and Gawber went out.

The phone rang. It was the civilian receptionist. 'There's a strange man on the phone. He says his name is Mr Love. Do you want to speak to him?'

'I certainly do. Please put him through.'

There was a click and the Irish voice said, 'Mr Angel? Are you there? At great personal risk I got that info you was wanting.'

'Shall we meet at the usual place?'

'Yus. Five o'clock all right? It'll be dark then.'

'All right. Goodbye.'

Outside, it was blacker than the Black Maria and twice as gloomy.

Angel had spent most of the day assembling paperwork for the CPS that was going to put Liam Quigley, Harry Savage and Hector Munro away for a substantial numbers of years. He was very regretful that it seemed that the small and chillingly alluring Felicity Santana was going to get away with all her crimes. Some you win, some you lose.

He noted the time. It was five minutes to five. He had an appointment with Mr Love at five o'clock. It was time to leave. He put on his coat, switched off the desk light and made for the door. He remembered something. He came back to his desk, pulled open the middle drawer, fished for the wage envelope Crisp had been awarded by the studio and tore it open. It contained £200 in £20 notes. He put £100 in his left pocket and £100 in his right. Then he looked round the room. Everything else could wait until tomorrow. He switched off the light, closed the door and dashed up the corridor.

When he arrived outside the station the cold hit him in the face like the opening of the fridge door in the mortuary. He went down the steps on to the pavement, crossed the road and stepped lively down the ginnel at the back of the Fat Duck to St Barnabas churchyard. He opened the iron gate and went in, just as the church clock chimed five.

'Mr Love,' he said into the dark. But there was no reply. He was surprised, but not concerned. He had always found Love reliable. He thought he may have been delayed in the New Year's Eve traffic or held up with the weather.

There was fog in the air and a few wisps weaved between the gravestones.

Angel rubbed his chin and wondered exactly what success Love had had. He fully expected that he would say that it was Munro who had bought the gun. That would further help strengthen the case against him, which would be perfect. If Love said that it was Samson Fairchild, that would be an embarrassment, because Angel had no other evidence to support a case against him. Love might even have discovered that it was Felicity Santana who had obtained the weapon for Munro to do the dirty work. But that wasn't likely. She was too smart for that.

He shrugged. Why was he worrying? To mount a prosecution, Twelvetrees had said that he only needed evidence to show Munro and Felicity Santana together. That must be possible, but the couple had been extremely discreet in that regard. Forensic would be ideal: DNA was indisputable.

There were footsteps behind him.

'Mr Angel,' a voice called out.

It was Love. 'Yes, Mr Love.'

'Ah. I'm sorry I wasn't waiting for you. Are you alone?'

'Indeed I am. Are you?'

'Of course. Perishing cold, it is.'

Angel heard the Irishman blow into his hands.

'Let's get this over with, Mr Angel. Did you bring the money?'

'Yes. Have you got the information? Were you able to find out who bought the Walther PPK/S – the one used to murder a man on 16 December?'

'Of course. And it is going to cost you £500.'

Angel gasped. 'Don't be ridiculous, Mr Love. This is public money. I haven't got that much, but even if I had you know I couldn't give it to you. It would set an impossible precedent. As it is, I'm breaking the law *now*. I should have your name and address in a book in the station, with every transaction, the information passed and the amount of cash paid duly recorded. I don't insist on that, but you've got to be reasonable. I don't even have your real name—'

'That is my real name.'

'I don't have your address.'

'You don't *need* my address. Anyway, what is this info worth to you, Mr Angel? Honestly now?'

'You know we coppers pay fifty quid tops, but this is a bit special. Honestly, £100.'

Angel heard Love spit into the dark. 'Sod you, Mr Angel. For me to preserve my life, it's worth more than £100 to keep this to myself. I was hoping to get the fare to see my dear mother at St Joseph's in Balley Ocarey, but you have been wasting my time.'

'Wait a moment, please, Mr Love,' Angel said. 'That information I said was honestly worth to me £100, no more, and that is so, but the continuance of your goodwill is worth a lot more than that. But I do happen to have another £100, so that I can give you £200.'

Mr Love grunted.

'Would that be enough to cover the risk you took in getting me this information – which I still require to be one hundred per cent reliable – and purchase you a ticket to St Joseph's in Balley Ocarey, and allow you a more than adequate Hogmanay celebration?'

Angel waited. He licked his lips. This was a tricky moment.

'My information is always one hundred per cent reliable, Mr Angel. You can take that for granted from me. I appreciate your candidness, though. All right. I accept your two hundred.'

In the dark they found each other's hands and eagerly shook them.

Angel thought Love's hand was like a piece of cod straight off the slab. Then Angel handed the money bundled together from both pockets.

'There's ten £20 notes,' Angel said.

Love stuffed it in his pockets, then he said, 'All you need from me is a name, but I give you more. The Walther gun was bought by Peter Santana, the millionaire fella, in the silver Mercedes car, on or about Monday 10 November. Now I hope you're satisfied.'

Angel gasped. 'That can't be right. He's the man who was murdered.'

'I tort you'd be surprised. Take it from me. It'll be right. Now I must be off. You know how to get in touch if you need me. Happy New Year, Mr Angel.'

'Happy New Year, Mr Love.'

'Good morning, sir, and a Happy New Year.'

Angel looked as if he'd just returned from a funeral. 'Come in, Ron. You don't have to be so bloody hearty.'

Gawber looked down at him and said, 'My sister, her husband and all their tribe are over for the day. He's got the day off. So I'm very glad to be out of it all. Anyway, I thought you were a well-known workaholic, sir. What's the matter?'

'Sit down. We might have got the wrong bloke. How did you get on yesterday?'

Gawber's mouth dropped open. 'The wrong bloke?' he said.

'What about Miss Freedman? And Doncaster?'

'That went all right, sir. The statement totally overturned Quigley's alibi.'

'And Munro?'

'Nothing spectacular,' Gawber said. 'I simply read the charge out to him.'

'And how did he react?'

'He shook his head vigorously. I waited a bit and then asked him if he'd anything to say. But he said nothing.'

Angel wrinkled his nose then told Gawber that a reliable source had told him that it was Peter Santana who had bought the Walther, back in November.

Gawber blinked. 'It couldn't have been.'

'That's what I said.'

'It had to be Hector Munro or Samson Fairchild.'

'Exactly.'

The pupils of Gawber's eyes moved uncertainly from side to side. 'Had Peter Santana worked out some devious suicide that has left Munro looking guilty of murder, sir?'

'I wondered that, at first … I can't make any sense of it. It would have been very fitting for him and Felicity if it *had been* like that. But I don't think so.'

'Is your informant reliable, sir? Could he have made a mistake?'

'He's always been reliable in the past, Ron. I don't see why he shouldn't be now. I don't know where to go with this.' There was a moment's quiet then Angel said: 'Supposing Santana did buy the gun. It could have been for his own protection. He's immensely rich, not physically strong, he could easily have been taken hostage for an enormous sum. We don't see many cases of it these days, but we know it sometimes happens.'

'And he was worrying about it? He was afraid.'

'Yes … and unaware that Munro was planning to murder him.'

'We don't know if Santana knew about his wife carrying on with Munro, sir?'

Angel rubbed his chin. 'No, we don't. But I expect he did.'

'Was there some symbolism involving the pig and the silk nightdress and the candlestick, sir?'

'I don't know, Ron. That's still a muddle. However, it has set me on an entirely new line of thought.'

Angel leaned back in the swivel chair and gazed at the ceiling. After a few moments he said, 'Have you written up your notes?'

'No, sir. Haven't had the opportunity.'

'Well, hop off and do it then. Leave me with this. I have to think this thing through….'

Gawber recognized the signs. He came out of the office and closed the door quietly.

CHAPTER 16

Two hours later, Angel banged open his office door, hitting the chair behind it. He went charging down the corridor to the CID office and stared inside. His hair was all over, his eyes staring, his tie loose and his top button unfastened.

PC Ahmed Ahaz, who was at his desk near the door, stared back at him. He thought he had been drinking.

Ahmed was worried. 'What's up, sir? Can I get you anything?'

'Yes, Ahmed. If Felicity Santana weighs 7 stone 2 lbs, I've solved it.'

'Would you like a cup of tea, sir?'

'I'll have a gallon of tea later, Ahmed. At the moment I need to know if Felicity Santana weighs 7 stone 2 lbs. I wonder … How can I find that out?'

Ahmed looked blank.

Angel turned away and went further down the corridor to Superintendent Harker's room. He grabbed the handle and walked in.

Harker was at his desk and looked up in surprise. Angel leaned over his desk, blinked through the camphor fumes and said, 'If Felicity Santana weighs 7 stone 2 lbs, I have solved the whole nonsense of the pink candles, the fuses, the ether, the silk nightdress, the petrol and the pig and everything.'

'I'm busy, Angel. Can't you see that? And you didn't knock.'

Ahmed came through the open door and hovered, wondering what to do.

Angel's lips tightened back against his teeth. 'How can I find out if she weighs 7 stone 2 lbs or not?'

Harker said: 'This is ridiculous.'

'You don't know, do you?' said Angel.

'From her passport,' Harker said.

'Ah!' Angel yelled. 'But we haven't got her passport, sir. Come on. Come on. Where else might we find out?'

Gawber appeared at the door. He must have heard the commotion.

Angel spotted him and ran over to him. 'Ron. Ron. I want to know if Felicity Santana weighs 7 stone 2 lbs. Where can I find that out quickly?'

Gawber looked bewildered.

'Her passport, her business manager, I suppose.'

Harker got up from behind his desk and, pushing Ahmed towards Angel, said: 'You can settle this somewhere else. Get out. All of you. I won't have this in my office. Go on. Get out. Shoo.'

Gawber got hold of Angel's arm and directed him out of the office. 'Come on, sir.'

'We're going, sir,' Ahmed said. 'Sorry, sir,' Ahmed added as he closed the superintendent's office door.

They were out in the corridor. Angel said, 'This is no good. I need to know her weight. That's all. Can't I make you understand?'

'Let's go back to your office, sir,' Gawber said, grabbing his arm.

'I can walk. I know the way.' Angel shrugged him off. 'You don't understand, Ron. I need to know her weight. The whole premise hinges on that. If it is 7 stone 2 lbs I have solved the whole puzzle. I know exactly why the pig was in a silk nightie.'

Gawber and Ahmed looked at each other.

'We could phone her up? Ask her,' Ahmed said.

Angel said, 'No.'

'Would her doctor know?' Gawber said.

Angel's eyes flashed. '*He'd know!* Yes. He'd know.'

They had arrived at Angel's office. He reached into his pocket and pulled out a used envelope. Scrawled in a corner was the name 'Prakash, Santana's GP, Bond Road, Tel 284845'.

Angel tapped in the number.

'Dr Prakash speaking.'

'DI Michael Angel, Bromersley police. Remember me? I am looking into Peter Santana's murder.'

'Oh yes, Inspector. What can I do for you?'

'I need something … It might seem strange to you, Doctor. I need to know the weight of Mrs Santana.'

'I beg your pardon? I thought you said you needed to know Mrs Santana's weight.'

'That's right. I thought you would have that information.'

There was some hesitation. 'This *is* for police business, isn't it? Not for some newspaper or magazine article or …'

Angel breathed in noisily then said, 'This is Detective Inspector Angel of the Bromersley force, Doctor. Do you not recognize my voice?'

'Very well, Inspector. I'll take a look at her records. Hold on.'

It seemed to take ages. Then Angel heard the doctor returning and picking up the phone. 'Mrs Santana had a check-up in August last, Inspector, and she weighed the same as she has for the last three years. That is 7 stone 2 lbs.'

Angel sighed then said, 'Thank you, Doctor. 7 stone 2 lbs. Thank you very much.'

He beamed, replaced the phone, leaned back in the chair and closed his eyes.

Ahmed said, 'Now would you like a cup of tea, sir?'

‘Yes, lad. Six sugars. And bring one for DS Gawber.’

Ahmed went out and closed the door.

‘It all fits like a jigsaw puzzle, Ron, without a piece missing,’ he said with a sigh. ‘It came to me when I reversed things … I mean … suppose Santana had been thinking of murdering Felicity? Should he tolerate her infidelity for ever? Of course not. I first began to suspect her when you told me that at that shop called Exotica, the assistant told you that Felicity had found out that her husband had bought a nightie. Now that’s bound to whip up a woman’s concern when a husband buys a sexy silk nightie and discovers it’s not for her.’

Gawber nodded. ‘Not half. Can imagine my wife’s reaction! Huh!’

‘But she never mentioned to me that she knew he had bought the nightie and that it was not for her,’ Angel said. ‘Not a word. Also she would naturally become concerned when she heard that her husband Peter was considering changing his will, when she had understood that already everything of his had been unconditionally left to her: a change, whatever it was, could only be worse. Anyway, the night of Santana’s murder was the night of the late filming, that was Monday, the fifteenth. Santana may have said that he would spend the night at the farmhouse, so she thought that it was a good night to set things in motion. She told Munro that Santana would be up there alone, promised him the moon with jam on it, gave him the gun, which I’ll go into later, and after they had finished filming, set him off up there. She allowed the studio driver to take her home to Creesforth Road to support her story. Munro parked the Range Rover a good distance away from the farmhouse, and walked up the hill. There is a trodden-down area by the drive gate where I expect he stood, possibly with binoculars, a few minutes. At about midnight, Munro tried the front door. It wasn’t locked so he went inside. The place was in darkness. Santana probably heard him. Munro went in the bedroom, found Santana coming towards him and shot him in the chest. Santana fell where we found him. Munro may have checked to see if he was dead, but probably not. Anyway, he kept his head, closed the doors, wiped his prints off the door handles and ran down the drive and out to his car at the bottom of the hill somewhere and drove home. Easy.'

There was a knock at the door. It was Ahmed with the tea, two cups and saucers on a black tin tray. Gawber smiled at him and took the tray.

'Thank you, Ahmed,' Angel said. He took one of the cups off the tray.

Ahmed went out and closed the door.

'Yes,' Angel said. 'I was saying that while Felicity and Munro were planning to kill him, he was, at the same time, also planning to get rid of Felicity. His plan was much more subtle than theirs. He was planning for it to seem like an accident. And in typical Santana style, he also intended making money out of it – £1.5 million.'

'That's a lot of money, sir. How?'

'I'll tell you, Ron. He had fallen out of love with the farmhouse … probably because primarily it was so cold up there. Of course he had plenty of heating inside, but I suppose there were no really warm days. Even when the sun was strong, the wind would blow any warmth away. Anyway, for whatever reason, he had had enough of the place. Felicity had stopped coming up there years back, even for a visit. So he doubled the insurance, and bought a can of petrol. What other use could he have had for petrol in the garage, when both of their cars run on diesel?'

Gawber, sipping the tea, looked up in realization.

'But his physical powers were waning. Felicity wasn't going to come to the farmhouse voluntarily, so he intended that she should come unconsciously. That's what he wanted the ether for.'

'But we didn't find any ether, sir,' Gawber said.

'No. He hadn't bought the ether yet. That night was only a rehearsal for him. An exercise to see if he could lift the unconscious Felicity, put a nightdress on her and so on.

He bought a pig exactly the same weight as Felicity, and a silk nightdress because he thought it would slide along her unconscious body easier than, say, cotton. He withdrew fuses and wiped them clean of his prints to suggest that there was something wrong with the electrics and provide an explanation as to why she would need to use candles. He would have covered the bed, with the unconscious Felicity in it, with a measured amount of petrol. He wouldn't want the place stinking of the stuff and thereby give the game away. Then he would have laid the candlestick close at hand, opened a few windows and doors and let mother nature do her worst.'

'Phew,' Gawber said. 'Some plan.'

Angel finished the tea and put the cup back in the saucer.

Gawber said: 'You didn't tell me about the Walther, sir.'

He nodded. 'My snout was right. Santana bought the gun – he said 10 November. More than a month ago. I think that he bought the gun for his own protection, probably put it in his desk or somewhere like that. Felicity found it, and when the time was right took it and gave it to Munro. After it had been used to murder Santana, Munro carefully wiped it clean of prints, but not down the tiny nooks and crannies, and dumped it in the gentlemen's washroom to widen the range of suspects.'

'Fantastic,' Gawber said, his face glowing. 'You've done it again.'

A knock at the door saved Angel's blushes. 'Come in.'

It was Scrivens. He was carrying a big plastic bag.

'What is it, lad?' Angel said, looking up.

Scrivens held open the bag. 'It's these tennis balls, sir. The ones we took from Laurence Smith's hut. They're still in my locker. I can't move for them. I want to know what to do with them. And you said you'd tell me about the tennis ball scam.'

Angel smiled. 'Very well. Listen up. In old property, such as the Victorian-built houses where Smith lives, the guttering and the pipes are a bit far seen into. If you're handy with a set of ladders, you can climb up on to the roofs of these houses and drop a tennis ball down each of the fall pipes. Then after the next heavy downfall of rain, there will be a whole street full of people with flooding problems, needing their pipes attending to. At the critical moment, you can knock on their door in overalls and carrying a bag of tools and, at today's prices, you can clean up about 300 quid a house. And you even get your ball back. Got it?'

Scrivens stood there, his eyes bright, his mouth slightly open. Eventually he said, 'Yes, sir. Thank you. I never knew that.'

Angel said: 'Right, lad. Now off you go.'

Scrivens stood his ground. 'Yes, sir, but what shall I do with these balls?'

Angel looked back at Gawber and said, 'The sergeant will tell you what to do with them, lad, won't you, Ron?'

Gawber stared at him.

The phone rang.

'Off you go. The pair of you. Sort him out, Ron, will you?' he said.

The door closed.

Angel picked up the phone. It was DS Taylor.

'Yes, Don?'

'I'm at Munro's house, sir. Thought you'd like to know that there are examples of female hair on the bedding that look very much like Felicity Santana's. Same colour, same texture as the samples taken from the hairbrush in her caravan at the studio.'

The bees started buzzing round in Angel's chest. 'Great stuff, Don.'

'There's more, sir.'

Angel was so excited he wasn't certain he could take any more. 'Yes?'

'Her fingerprints are all over the shower door and the taps.'

He replaced the phone.

He had a smile as big as the sun.

The BMW seemed to drive itself to Angel's house and into his garage.

He locked the garage door and let himself in the back door.

Mary called out from somewhere in the sitting room. 'Hello. Is that you, love?'

'No,' he called back, then assumed the gruff voice of a pantomime villain. 'It's that big, bad womanizer from Bromersley nick, and I'm coming to get you!'

She pretended to scream and spoke an octave higher. 'Oh! No. No. I'm only thirteen.'

'I'm not superstitious,' he growled.

'But my mother wouldn't *like* it,' she said.

'Your mother's not going to *get* it.'

'I'll tell the *vicar*.'

'I *am* the vicar,' he said and he arrived in the room with a beer he had taken from the fridge en route and looked round for her.

She was seated in the chair, reading a book.

'You silly fool,' she said with a big smile. 'You're in a good mood.'

He leaned over and gave her a big kiss on the lips.

'You've solved the pig in the bed thing?' she said.

He lifted up his head and said: 'Yes.'

'And you want to tell me about it.'

'No,' he lied. '*Not* if you don't want to know about it.'

'I do. I do. I want to know *all* about it,' she lied. 'But—' She suddenly looked very sternly at him. 'There is something very important that we have to deal with first.'

He frowned then sipped the beer. His mind raced round, trying to think what it was.

Her face was as straight as a Bible. 'Look at you,' she said. 'You've forgotten already.'

He screwed up his eyes. 'What?' he said.

'You've forgotten about little Timmy's wedding present. The wedding's next week. We've *got* to send them something … something really nice.'

It suddenly dawned on him what she was talking about. 'Oh yes,' he said. 'Of course. All taken care of.'

She looked at him closely, her mouth dropping open.

'I thought about a Swiss clock,' he said.

Her face brightened. She smiled. 'That sounds … nice, Michael. Expensive.'

'A cuckoo clock.'

'Unusual.'

'Yes,' Angel said. 'As it happens I've bought one. It's in the car. Already boxed up.'

Mary beamed at him.

He smiled back at her and emptied the glass of beer.

THE END

OTHER BOOKS BY ROGER SILVERWOOD

YORKSHIRE MURDER MYSTERIES

Book 1: THE MISSING NURSE
Book 2: THE MISSING WIFE
Book 3: THE MAN IN THE PINK SUIT
Book 4: THE MORALS OF A MURDERER
Book 5: THE AUCTION MURDERS
Book 6: THE MISSING KILLER
Book 7: THE UMBRELLA MURDERS
Book 8: THE MISSING MILLIONAIRE
Book 9: THE MISSING THIEF
Book 10: FIND THE LADY
Book 11: THE MISSING MODEL
Book 12: MURDER IN BARE FEET
Book 13: THE MISSING HUSBAND
Book 14: THE CUCKOO CLOCK MURDERS

Printed in Great Britain
by Amazon

78907807R00113